The Albatross

The Albatross Conspiracy

James Jauncey

ANDRE DEUTSCH

First published in 1990 by
André Deutsch Limited
105 – 106 Great Russell Street, London WC1B 3LJ

British Library Cataloguing in Publication Data

Jauncey, James
  The albatross conspiracy.
  I. Title
  823.914 [F]

ISBN 0 233 98585 9

Phototypeset by AKM Associates (UK) Ltd
Ajmal House, Hayes Road, Southall, London
Printed and bound in Great Britain by
WBC, Bristol and Maesteg

Chapter 1

There were four of them. They wore dark overalls and boots, heavy gloves and black balaclavas. A trained observer would scarcely have spotted the pale ovals of eyes and mouths against the moonless hillside.

They climbed out of a dip and paused on a ridge. Below them winked a scattering of lights, reflected dully in the long ribbon of loch.

'There she is!' The speaker's voice was high-pitched and nasal. His breath clouded on the night air as he pointed to the outline of a fenced factory compound at the outskirts of the small town. 'Ready and waiting!'

'For the PAA!' There was a younger man's laugh, short and nervous. 'Come on then, let's do it.'

They set off again, picking their way silently and carefully down the broken, heathered terrain of the hillside.

It would be easy, there was no question of that. Apart from one elderly security guard, most likely dozing in the gatehouse, their target was not protected, had no need to be. No one knew they were coming. No one had ever heard of them — so far.

Tomorrow it would be a different story. Front page news. The People's Army of Alba. A new force for independence.

This was the tension that pumped the adrenalin through four sets of arteries. The tension of the first strike.

The ground was levelling now. A hundred yards ahead lay the road. A little way beyond it rose the wire fence with the silhouettes of large worksheds looming behind. A single pool of light spilled from the gatehouse. Otherwise the place was in darkness.

They were almost at the road when the feeble glow of a bicycle lamp became visible, weaving from side to side as it headed towards them from the town.

'Down!' all four threw themselves flat in the heather.

Now they could hear the rider of the bicycle singing tunelessly, drunkenly. The bicycle squeaked and rattled in rhythmic complaint.

'From the Invercarron Hotel.' It was the smallest of the four. 'They keep the bar open late during the lambing.'

'I've been a wild rover for many a year . . .'

The bicyclist was almost level with them.

'. . . I've spent all my money on whisky and . . . whoo-oops . . .' There was a clatter and a thump and the sound of breaking glass. 'Ouf . . . ow . . . oh, buggeration . . .' Whisky fumes drifted towards them.

The nervous one shook his head impatiently in the darkness. 'Bloody drunks!'

The bicyclist picked himself up off the road, righted the bicycle and climbed back onto it. He pedalled off erratically, muttering.

'We could've walked right in front of him and he'd not've seen us,' said the small one scornfully, as the lamp dwindled down the road.

'Aye, we could that,' came the nasal reply. 'Better safe, though . . .'

For a moment they waited to see whether the security guard would respond to the disturbance. But nothing stirred in the gatehouse. They slipped across the road, then set off down the side of the fence.

Fifty yards further along, a burn ran out of the factory

grounds, passing under the fence in a concrete culvert on its way down to the loch. The short tunnel was built to accommodate the burn in full spate with room to spare. Now there was no more than a foot or so of black, peaty water swirling through it. The first three splashed through easily enough, bowed at the waist.

The fourth, an immense, silent man with a heavy beard, ran into difficulty when the backpack he was carrying snagged on the entrance to the tunnel, but he freed himself and stumbled through, bent almost double, the water licking at his knees.

With another quick glance at the gatehouse they sprinted across twenty yards of grass and halted, panting, in the shadow of the largest of three sheds. The large man unslung his backpack and gingerly distributed its contents to the others.

'OK,' whispered the leader. 'Stand by to synchronise timers. Three, two, one, now!' Each man clicked the hands of an identical alarm clock to midnight. 'Right, off we go. Back here in eight minutes.'

While the other three disappeared into the darkness, the large man slipped off his gloves and bent down at the base of the steel pillar which formed one corner support of the shed. Breathing heavily with concentration he moulded a large pat of pale, puttyish material against the steel. Then he pushed into it a silver cylinder, about twice the size of an ordinary electrical fuse.

From this trailed two lengths of wire, one of which he attached to one terminal of a small battery, the other to the minute hand of the alarm clock whose glass face had been removed. Finally he wired the other battery terminal to a metal pin which had been glued to the face of the clock at the three o'clock position. At twelve-fifteen the minute hand would meet the pin and the circuit would be completed.

He straightened up with a grunt of satisfaction and at that moment a door slammed. He shrank back into the shadows as the sound of footsteps and cheerful whistling approached.

3

A flashlight beam wavered over the ground, drawing closer. The large man stiffened. His huge fingers began to flex restlessly.

Now the flashlight was only a few yards away and he was rising onto the balls of his feet when a hand came down hard on his shoulder from the darkness behind him. He spun round to see deep-set eyes glaring at him. 'No! That is *not* our game!' came the whispered rebuke.

He stepped back, reluctantly, and flattened himself against the side of the shed as the security guard sauntered into view, still whistling and playing his flashlight idly over the grass.

Disinterested, or apprehensive at what he might find if he did his job properly, the guard gave the beam one careless flick into the shadows between the two sheds and passed by.

Twelve-ten. The other two had not yet joined them. They could hear the guard's whistling from somewhere at the back of the third shed. He had stopped, probably for a pee. The other two wouldn't move till he was well past them, almost back at the gatehouse.

'Could we not just go?' There was an edge to the large man's voice.

'No! We wait for them.'

Twelve-twelve. The whistling was moving slowly down the far end. They were big sheds, admittedly. But, by God, he was taking his time.

Twelve-thirteen. A third figure slipped up beside them. It was the smallest of the four. 'OK, let's go, let's go!'

'What about . . . ?'

'He's coming . . . down the other side. C'mon, we gotta get outa here.'

They broke cover and sprinted for the burn.

As they reached the culvert an angry yell echoed between the sheds: 'Hey you! Stop!'

The fourth man burst into the open, followed shortly by the security guard.

Now the first three were emerging on the far side of the

tunnel. They threw themselves down on the ground as their companion splashed into the burn behind them.

Then came the explosion.

It plucked the security guard from his feet and tossed him fifteen yards down the grass where he lay still, arms and legs akimbo.

It roared through the concrete culvert, sucking the air from the fourth man's lungs as it hurled him face down in the water.

It flattened the other three against the heather and when it had passed they lifted their heads to see gouts of flame and clouds of black smoke seething into the night sky. The shed was unrecognisable — a charnel-house of shattered concrete, twisted steel and steaming, sundered machinery.

The fourth man picked himself up from the water and staggered out of the culvert, blood streaming from a deep gash in his left wrist.

He stopped by his companions and turned to gaze for a moment at their night's work.

Then, as lights came on in the town, doors were thrown open and telephones began to ring, the four men slipped back across the road and melted away onto the darkened hillside.

Chapter 2

Christie sat in the kitchen of her grandmother's cottage staring without inspiration at the blank page of a diary.

She had promised herself that today she would bring the neglected diary up to date. It was a school holiday project which had started well; but as soon as she had arrived at Mellon Udrigle, the lure of the beach had overtaken her and her good intentions had evaporated.

She sucked her pen and drummed her fingers in time with the music coming from the old radio that stood on the dresser.

Step we gaily, on we go / Heel for heel and toe for toe / Arm in arm and row on row / All for Mairi's wedding . . . The breezing lilt of *The Lewis Bridal Song* filled the kitchen. Christie put down the pen and hummed along with it.

Now it's nine-thirty, came the presenter's voice as the song ended, *and over to Robbie Donald in the newsroom.*

Responsibility for yesterday's bombing of the Anglo Printing Group's Invercarron paper mill has been claimed by a group of extreme Scottish nationalists calling themselves The People's Army of Alba. In a letter received by The Scotsman *this morning, the PAA have stated that the bombing was 'a first blow for the people of Scotland against their political, economic and ecological oppressors, the English.' Damage to the mill is estimated at several hundred thousand pounds. One employee is now in hospital being treated for concussion. Otherwise no one was hurt. Little is yet known about the PAA and police have mounted a full-scale investigation . . .*

She got up and switched it off. Remote and sheltered in this little West Highland hamlet, it seemed to Christie that the news was a brutal and quite unnecessary intrusion by the outside world, especially when it brought tales of doom and destruction.

She looked out of the window, then glanced down at the diary and flipped it shut. It was a glorious day and the diary could wait. Maybe she'd wander over to *Loch na Beiste* and see if Kenny Tulloch was working at the salmon hatchery.

'I'm going out, Nan,' she said, poking her head round the sitting room door.

'All right, dear. See you later.'

Leaving the cottage she set off along the road that skirted the beach and led back along the treeless, hummocky peninsula towards the mainland. To her left, beyond the beach and Mellon Udrigle's little bay lay the much larger Gruinard Bay, a deep blue in the April sunshine. Beyond that, rising like a row of white anvils on the horizon, were the great hills of Sutherland and Wester Ross with their magical Gaelic names: *Suilven, Stac Pollaidh, Ben Mor Coigach, Beinn Ghobhlach, Sail Mhor, An Teallach.*

While the snow was still on them the cold season was not truly over and winter could return at any moment. For the time being, however, spring was here with a gentle breeze and the light strong and clear.

As she crested the hill beyond the beach, Christie was pleased to see Kenny Tulloch's white landrover parked down by the small loch which lay below her.

Kenny was a large and cheerful man with thick white eyebrows and a broken nose. He worked for Gairloch Salmon, one of several companies which had turned the salmon farming into big business over recent years. Christie had come to know him quite well and sometimes went out in the boat with him to the hatchery, whose rectangular aluminium frame and pink fluorescent buoys bobbed distinctively in the middle of the loch. She enjoyed seeing the water boil as it was sprinkled with feed and she loved the way the light caught the scales of the wriggling, smoky-blue parr as Kenny weighed and measured them.

She wandered down to the landrover, looking forward to a chat and maybe a cup of tea — he always had a thermos with him. But the landrover was empty. The boat was moored to the jetty and Kenny was nowhere to be seen.

She tried the passenger door. It was open so she climbed in. Kenny wouldn't mind. He couldn't have gone far. She made herself comfortable and looked round for the canvas bag which usually held the thermos. It didn't seem to be there.

Ten minutes passed and she was beginning to wonder where he could have got to when something dark broke the surface by the jetty. A moment later a black-clad figure heaved itself out of the water, stood up and began to unsling a yellow oxygen tank from its back. It was too small to be Kenny, she realised. She scrambled from the landrover as it walked towards her, peeling off a mask and a black hood.

'Oy! What were you doing in there?' The voice was belligerent.

'I'm sorry. I thought it was . . .'

'I don't care what you thought it was. You'd no business in that landrover.' He was about thirty, medium-height and starting to bald. He looked at her suspiciously through narrow, greenish-grey eyes.

'Look,' said Christie, 'I said I'm sorry. I thought it was Kenny Tulloch's. I'm a friend of his.'

'Are you now,' he said briskly. 'Well, it is Kenny's as a matter of fact. Mine's off the road. I've got twenty-five cage inspections to do in the next ten days and I can't wait till it's fixed. Now, if you don't mind . . .'

Rude so-and-so, she thought. Most people up here were only too pleased to stop for a natter. As much to annoy him as anything else she asked a question:

'Is this one all right, then?' She pointed out to the cage.

His eyes narrowed again as he answered: 'Yes, yes, it's fine. Why do you want to know?'

Christie shrugged. 'No reason . . . But I thought that you never dived alone, just in case . . . I mean . . . isn't it dangerous?'

'You ask a lot of questions.'

'Just curious, that's all.'

'Well, Miss Curious, if you really want to know, I was ten years on the North Sea rigs and I'll tell you, after that, these wee lochs are a piece of cake. This one's only about ten feet deep at the deepest. Safe as houses. And I'll live to be forty.'

He turned away and moved to the back of the landrover, unzipping the sleeves of the wet-suit. Christie caught a glimpse of bandage around his left wrist as she set off towards the road.

She had gone twenty yards when there was a loud 'Bloody hell!' behind her. She turned to see a stream of papers being plucked from the open tailgate of the landrover by the breeze. The diver was dashing after them like a retriever, cursing as he snatched them from the heather.

Christie hesitated for a moment, then ran after him and gathered half a dozen sheets of what appeared to be cage inspection report forms. He took them from her, then turned away and leant against the landrover, frowning anxiously as he flicked through the sheaf of papers.

After a few moments he slammed his fist furiously against the bonnet, brushed past her and strode across the heather, scanning the ground intensely.

At first Christie was too startled to speak. Then she called after him: 'D'you want a hand?' But her offer went unacknowledged.

'Can I help?' she called again, starting to run after him. This time he shook his head without turning round so she made her way up to the road and set off back towards Mellon Udrigle.

It wasn't just that he was unfriendly, she thought, as she walked slowly up the hill again. There was something nervous, almost . . . paranoid about him. Still, you'd have to be pretty odd to want to be a diver in the first place, especially out in the North Sea. A schoolfriend's uncle was a diver and she'd heard some real horror stories about what went on beneath the rigs . . .

A dirty grey estate car appeared over the brow of the hill, going too fast for single-track road. Christie leapt for the heathery bank at the roadside, missed her footing and tumbled down into the drainage ditch. The car screeched to a halt and reversed towards her.

The driver wound down the window and peered out. He was middle-aged and dark-haired with a long, melancholy face and deep-set eyes astride a curving beak of a nose.

'Are you all right, lassie?' The voice was high-pitched and nasal.

'Yes, yes I think so,' she called back shakily.

'Well, you should look where you're going.' He wound up the window and drove off.

'*You* should look, you creep,' she muttered, scrambling out of the ditch. She stood at the roadside dusting herself down. Now the car had stopped at *Loch na Beiste*. The driver and the diver held a brief conversation, then the car sped off again.

Christie made her way over the hill and down towards the beach with the white cottages clustered at its far end. It didn't surprise her that the two men knew each other. Birds of a distinctly creepish feather, she thought angrily.

She crossed the sandy turf which encircled the beach and headed for her favourite reading place, at the foot of one of the dunes. She climbed up the back of it, slithering on the fine white sand and stopped at the top. Damn it! The boy was there, watching her again. That was all she needed.

She had seen him for the first time yesterday, slouched against the drystone dyke of the little field as she helped her grandmother feed the blackfaced ewes and their lambs from a bucket. His shoulders drooped and his arms dangled awkwardly at his sides, as if he didn't know what to do with them. She knew he had been watching her for the couple of times she had caught his eye he had immediately lowered his gaze. Eventually he had sauntered off, rattling a stick along the uneven surface of the wall. The noise had infuriated her.

Now he was sitting on an upturned boat, twenty yards away. His head was cupped in both hands, his elbows resting on his knees as his feet scuffed idle patterns in the sand. Slim, almost skinny, he was wearing frayed jeans and an over-large red sweatshirt which jarred against a shimmer of close-cropped ginger hair.

There was an air of dejection and boredom about him that she found profoundly irritating. If he couldn't appreciate this place, especially on such a wonderful spring day, he should push off.

She dropped to the foot of the dune, out of his sight, and sat down with a sigh. Everyone seemed to be annoying her this afternoon. For a while she gazed at the bay, then pulled her book from her coat pocket and began reading.

Some time later a large herring gull flapped onto the sand in front of her. It folded its grey wings along its back, cocked its head to scrutinise her, then turned its attention to a crab shell. Almost immediately something thumped into the sand behind it. The gull squawked indignantly and took to the air, twisting suddenly as another stone sailed past it. There was a soft thud behind Christie's head and a trickle of sand ran down her neck.

She got to her feet and walked towards the boy who had assembled a small arsenal of stones on the hull of the boat beside him.

'Hey!' she said angrily. 'You nearly hit me!'

The boy shrugged and turned to stare out across the bay.

'You shouldn't be throwing stones at birds, anyway. What harm did it do you?'

The boy continued to ignore her.

'I said what harm did it do you?' she demanded. She

wasn't going to let him get away with it.

'It was a black-back,' he replied at length, still facing away from her. 'My dad says they're brutes. They eat other birds' eggs and chicks.' His accent was from the south, Dundee perhaps.

'Your dad's right. But you're wrong. That wasn't a black-back, it was a herring gull. The blackies are much bigger and darker. You should know your birds better before you start chucking things at them.'

'You're pretty clever, aren't you.' He turned to face her now, angry flushes spreading across his cheeks. His skin was pale, the eyelids almost translucent between the sandy eyebrows and eyelashes. 'That wasn't a black-back, that was a herring-gull.' He imitated her West Highland lilt, making it sound prim and self-righteous.

Christie blushed. 'Haven't you got anything better to do, then?'

He shrugged again. 'Nope.'

'Well perhaps you'd mind not throwing stones at me. I'm trying to read.'

She turned away and walked back to the dune, settled onto the sand and picked up her book. But she was unable to concentrate for now a dull, hollow thumping had begun.

Exasperated, she rose and climbed the dune again. The boy's feet were drumming a monotonous tattoo against the hull as he lobbed his stones half-heartedly down the beach towards the water. He glanced round at her but his heels continued their assault on the boat and he showed no signs of moving.

For a moment Christie deliberated. All she wanted was a bit of peace and quiet in the sunshine. She didn't feel like returning to the cottage yet. That left only one alternative. She set off across the beach towards the old burial ground.

At the opposite end of the beach from the cottages were four modern, pine-built holiday cabins. They were set back amongst a belt of fir trees, their large, aluminium-framed picture windows facing across the bay. This was where he'd be staying, most likely, she thought, as she drew level with them. And it would probably be a real mess, the one he was in, with clothes all over the place and unwashed dishes in the sink.

Resisting the temptation to peer in the windows, she walked on past the cabins to the headland beyond. There, enclosed by a stone wall and perched on the edge of low cliffs, lay the burial ground. She opened the wrought-iron gate, slipped through and closed it behind her. She made her way over to the ruined church, no bigger than a cottage, that stood in the centre, and sat down with her back to its crumbling wall.

This was one place where she knew she would not be disturbed. The only other person who ever came here was a silent, ferret-like man from the District Council who turned up once in a while with a lawn mower in the back of a battered pick-up.

He wouldn't be coming today. The grass was recently-mown, a vibrant green in the sunlight, duller in the shadows cast by the headstones. Clumps of daffodils waved gently here and there in the breeze and a rabbit nibbled a dock leaf by a small patch of nettles.

She closed her eyes and breathed in deeply, letting the solitude of the place wash through her. What was happening today? What on earth had she done to deserve so much rudeness in one afternoon? First the diver, then that moron in the estate car, then the boy. And she was only trying to mind her own business and enjoy the good weather while it lasted. She was due back at home next Monday and it was already Wednesday . . .

The put-put of an approaching outboard intruded on her reverie. She stood up and walked over to the far wall, noticing as she did so that the movement was making her feel curiously light-headed. Nosing round the headland before her was a white fibreglass dinghy, probably from the hotel at Laide. A man sat at the tiller and in the bows a small boy was hauling in a line.

Now the boat turned into the bay. When it was no more than thirty yards from the beach the man cut the engine and stood up. At the same time the boy shifted across the bows to clear a snag in the line, the boat rocked slightly, the man lost his balance and the next moment the boat overturned.

Visitors, no doubt, she thought, as the boat settled keel up in the water. He should never have stood up in a boat that small. They'd be horribly cold in there, but it wasn't far to swim.

The man's head broke the surface and he shook it like a dog as he trod water for a moment, looking to right and left. The boat lay almost at right angles to him and it was clear he could not see its far side. Nor, from where she stood, could Christie. He set off around the stern, calling the boy's name, Michael, as he swam.

For a short while he was lost to veiw. Then he reappeared and Christie began to sense that the situation had altered. Now he was threshing the water with a panicky crawl which carried him a few yards out beyond the bows where he halted and duck-dived out of sight. Seconds later he resurfaced, swam another few paces and dived again.

She turned and dashed across the burial ground. Leaving the gate swinging open, she pounded back across the headland, past the trees and the cabins and down towards the near end of the beach where her grandmother's neighbour, Neil Cameron, kept his dinghy at the mouth of a small burn which flowed out across the sand. Neil's dinghy also was fibreglass and light enough for her to drag to the water if the tide wasn't too far out — she'd done it before.

She panted up a dune, praying the boat would be waiting where it usually was, and slithered down the other side towards the burn. The boat was there, tied to an iron rod set in a lump of concrete. She slipped the knot and began to heave the bows round to face the water — then stopped.

The bay was empty. The blue, sunlit water rippled gently, its surface unblemished by boat, man or boy. She sat down heavily on the sand, her breath rasping. She closed her eyes and opened them again. There was nothing.

Christie felt suddenly shaky and drained, as if all her energy was seeping out through the ends of her toes and soaking into the sand, like the water of the little burn beside her. She put her chin in her hands and stared blankly across the bay.

From somewhere amongst the heathery hillocks of the peninsula behind her came the throaty chuckle of a grouse, mocking her it seemed.

Chapter 3

'I've to go to Inverness tomorrow. I don't suppose you'll want to come with me?'

'I don't think so, thank you, Nan. I've only a few days left. I'd rather stay.'

'I thought as much. The time always passes so quickly when you're here.'

'I know,' said Christie, getting up from the table to clear away the plates. She squirted detergent into the plastic basin that sat in the sink, turned on the tap and watched as a soap bubble floated upwards, shimmering in the sunlight that streamed through the kitchen window.

Although it was seven o'clock in the evening the sun would not set for at least another hour yet. They were on the same latitude here as northern Labrador and only a little south of Leningrad, her grandmother had once shown her, tracing the line across the spread pages of an old atlas. In mid-summer you could read a book outdoors at midnight . . .

'I saw that young lad again, the one who was here last evening.' There was the creak of a chair as her grandmother rose from the table.

'Yes,' said Christie, putting the plates into the soapy

water. 'He was down on the beach this afternoon. Throwing stones at seagulls. He nearly hit me.'

'Did he now. He looked a poor sort of a thing to me. Lost, you might say.'

'I wish he'd got lost,' muttered Christie, half to herself. She scrubbed furiously at a plate, ready to blame the boy for everything — for spoiling her reading, for sending her to the burial ground, for the strange thing that had happened there and for the even stranger mood in which she now found herself.

'Is that what you told him?'

'No, but I wish I had.' She turned to face her grandmother. 'He was annoying me. I had to leave the beach. I went to the burial ground to get away from him.'

Her grandmother was silent for a moment. Then: 'You came back in an awful hurry.' She gave Christie a curious look, quizzical yet amused.

Christie blushed. 'I'd left my book on the beach and I wanted to get it before the tide came in,' she said lamely.

Her grandmother nodded and smiled, gracefully accepting the lie. Annoying as she sometimes found her grandmother's powers of observation, Christie could not suppress the sudden rush of affecton for the familiar white-haired figure in her cardigan, tweed skirt and wellingtons who stood with her blue-veined hands spread across the back of a kitchen chair.

'Well, you'd best get used to that laddie. He's going to be around for a day or two,' said her grandmother picking up her headscarf and making for the door. 'He's staying in one of the cabins with his dad. They're from down Blairgowrie way and they're here for a week while his dad fishes the Ewe. Now, I must go and see if Neil's in. I think Shona's lamb is on the way. She's looking a wee bit uncomfortable and I might need a hand. Come and join us when you're ready.'

'OK,' said Christie. 'But how d'you know . . . about the boy, I mean?'

'Willie told me,' came the reply as her grandmother left the room.

Christie nodded to herself. The visitors bought their provisions in Laide and were quizzed by Janet Bain, the elderly spinster who ran the post-office-cum-general store. Janet relayed her intelligence to Willie McLeod the postman. Willie, in the course of his round, would pass it on to Neil Cameron, or to Isobel McLaren or the Thompsons in the cottages on either side, or maybe to Nan herself. And so the news came full circle, back to Mellon Udrigle.

So who else had noticed her headlong dash to the beach this afternoon, she wondered, rinsing the plates and putting them in the drying rack? No one, probably. Neil would have been at work and both Isobel and the Thompsons were away over Easter.

It wouldn't have mattered, anyway. What did matter was trying to make sense of what had happened and why she was now feeling as she did. It was as if something quite unknown to her had stirred in some dim, distant inner recess. She found herself picturing a dark shape uncoiling somewhere deep within a mountain, getting to its feet and stretching — a dragon, perhaps, ancient and shadowy and unpredictable . . .

She finished the plates, wiped the table and went outside. Her grandmother and Neil Cameron, a stocky red-faced man with a tangle of greying curls, were talking at his front door.

'. . . a terrible thing, that explosion yesterday,' her grandmother was saying. 'Just senseless, senseless . . .'

'I know, and they said on the news this evening that this PAA, or whatever it's called, might be from around these parts. Imagine it, they'll be blowing up the fuel dump at Aultbea next. That's what I'd go for. It'll be a sitting duck now with all these MOD security cuts . . . Oh, hello there, Christie.' Neil gave her a cheerful smile. 'Your nan and I were just talking about this bombing at Invercarron.'

'Hello Neil . . . yes, I know. I heard it on the radio this morning.'

'Well now, are you coming to help us with Shona?'

Christie hesitated. Normally she would have been eager to attend the birth of a lamb — the miracle never failed to astound and delight her, especially when the mother was Shona, her grandmother's pet. But suddenly she felt the need to be alone with this strange and unfamiliar mood.

She glanced at her grandmother. 'Actually, Nan, if you don't mind I'd like to go for a walk while it's still light. Is that OK? You can manage, the two of you?'

Her grandmother looked at her askance for a moment, then smiled and said: 'Yes, dear, we'll manage. Off you go.'

'Aye well, we'll make a crofter of you yet, lassie,' said Neil with a good-natured chuckle. 'Enjoy your walk, now,'

'I will. And good luck with Shona.' She made her way round the back of the cottage and set off towards the end of the peninsula.

As she tramped through the heather, dodging the deeper peat-hags, she allowed the incident to replay itself over and over again in her mind. She had been walking for ten minutes or so when she found herself beginning to wonder whether it could have been anything to do with the book she was reading.

The Druid Saint had been a surprising choice, she had to admit. But it had seemed to draw her hand towards it as she had ranged the bookshelf in her grandmother's sitting room, the night she had arrived; and now, half-way through, she was completely absorbed by it. In fact, she was becoming aware of something curiously familiar about the story it told.

It was about Saint Columba, the Irish poet-priest, who had arrived on the island of Iona in AD 563, so bringing Christianity to Scotland. But it was not his successes with the heathen Picts that fascinated her; it was the misty world of the Druids, with their spells and potions, their astrology and human sacrifice and secret ritual, their epic poems and wild music. For the Druids had raised him and some of their ways had remained with him long after he had forsaken the ancient religion for the freezing monasteries and shaven monks, the tolling bells and chanted psalms of the new.

Columba's ability to see into the future was the thing that intrigued Christie the most. For example, the summer's night when he and his travelling companions had been sleeping out in the heather. Sometime around midnight he'd woken up with a vision of burning buildings so strong in his mind that he could almost smell the smoke.

He'd roused his monks and told them to go down to the village where they'd moored that evening and move the boat along the shore, away from the houses. Surprised and somewhat annoyed at being woken up, the monks nonetheless had done what he asked. Then they'd returned and gone back to sleep.

Just before dawn Columba had woken them again and told them to go back to the village. When they were still some way off they'd begun to see an orange glow in the sky and hear the crackle of burning timbers. The place was in flames . . .

Could that be what had happened to her, this afternoon? Could she have seen something that had yet to take place? She shook her head. Wishful thinking. And anyway, if this uneasy, dragon-like stirring inside her was anything to do with it, she'd be quite happy to have imagined the whole thing. Yes. Her seeing things before they happened was about as likely as . . . as those terrorists dropping in for a cup of tea.

By now she had reached the point. Here the land ended in a knuckled fist of sandstone which thrust into the sea. Below it, to the left, was a short strip of shingle beach broken by fingers of black, seaweed-covered rock.

Christie dropped down onto the shingle. She made her way out along the rocks, sat down and gazed around her. The sea was flat calm and turning quickly to molten silver as the sun inched its way down. At the far end of the beach an oyster-catcher waded at the waterline, probing with its long flame-coloured beak.

There was the faintest sound, hardly even a splash, as a sleek round head broke the surface, ten yards out from the shore. Water dripped from the whiskers and a pair of large, liquid eyes stared at her.

Christie sat perfectly still. Plop. The head disappeared, the water rippled, then it re-appeared, closer now. A moment later another, smaller head appeared beside the first. Two pairs of shiny black eyes regarded her inquisitively from the water.

'Hello, seals,' Christie said.

The smaller of the two turned its head a full circle, as if it had performed an invisible pirouette on the tip of its tail. Then it submerged and popped up again on the other side of its companion which had not moved.

There was a dull clatter behind her. Startled, the seals vanished. Christie looked around to see a blue object about the size of a large plate lying on the shingle. A frisbee. She began walking towards it when into view on the top of the headland sauntered the boy. A Walkman dangled at his waist, the headphones clamped to his ears.

Furious, Christie picked up the frisbee and held it in her hands for a moment, deliberating. Then she grasped it by the rim with her right hand and drew her right arm across her body.

'Hey!' He was pounding down the slope to the beach. Too bad. She flung it as hard as she could and watched with satisfaction as it sailed out over the water.

'What did you do that for?' He stopped in front of her, panting, his eyes wide with surprise.

'You frightened the seals away.'

'What seals? I don't see any seals.' He slipped the earphones round his neck where they buzzed tinnily, insistently.

'That's because they've gone now.'

'Maybe they'll come back.'

'I doubt it, not once they've been scared. Look, why don't you just go away and leave me alone.'

'Is this your beach?' His pale cheeks were reddening.

'No, of course not.'

'Well, I've as much right to be here as you. Perhaps I'll just wait here until the seals do come back.' He sat down and put the headphones on again.

Christie could feel her anger rising. She moved round and squatted down in front of him, her eyes level with his.

'You were following me, weren't you,' she bellowed. The boy rolled his eyes and put his hands to his ears. Then with exaggerated weariness he switched off the tape and removed the headphones once more.

'So what if I was?'

'I don't like being followed. Do you?'

He shrugged and flicked a pebble into the water. 'I hate this place. It's the most boring place I've ever been. There's nothing to do.'

'Then why don't you go fishing with your dad?'

'How . . . how d'you know that?'

'I just do. Never mind how. Anyway, why don't you?'

'Because it's even more boring than being here, if you really want to know. And . . . I don't get on with my dad.'

'Well, if it's my company you're after, you can forget it.'

'I never said it was.'

'So why were you following me?'

The boy got to his feet without replying and strolled over towards the rocks. The tide had carried the frisbee to within a few feet of their tip.

Infuriated, Christie turned on her heel and marched across the shingle. She was halfway up the bank when there was a yell and a loud splash. She turned round to see the boy floundering in the water off the end of the rocks, the frisbee grasped in one hand.

It was on the tip of her tongue to yell 'Serve you right' but his cry came first: 'Help, I can't swim!'

He's putting it on, she thought.

'Help! I'm drowning!'

He was starting to flail the water with his arms.

'Help me, please!'

There was real panic in the voice now.

Christie dashed back down the slope and across the beach. Twice in one day, she thought as she ran, but this time it's real. What an idiot! She scrambled over the rocks and plunged into the water beside him, gasping as the cold hit her.

The water was deep and the boy was struggling to keep his head up, thrashing with both arms, spitting and choking. Christie trod water beside him for a moment, then grabbed the neck of his sweatshirt and struck out for the rocks. They were no more than six feet away but the boy was flailing so hard that for a moment she thought he would pull her under. She kicked as hard as she could and at the same time heaved on the sweatshirt.

Her outstretched fingers touched something solid, she gave another kick with her legs and was able to hook her arm around a rock. With one more heave the boy's arm also flapped against the rock, he twisted in the water, took hold and began to haul himself out. Christie followed, stood up and led him back to the beach where he sat down heavily, shivering and dribbling streams of salt water.

After a while his shoulders stopped heaving and he wiped his face with the back of his hand. With his eyes fixed on the ground between his feet he muttered faintly: 'Thanks.'

'That's OK,' said Christie, hoping she didn't sound too sympathetic. 'Come on now, we'd better get home before we both get pneumonia.' Her sodden clothes clung to her like a film of ice and her teeth were starting to chatter.

The boy didn't move so she lent down and tapped him on the shoulder. 'You can't sit here all night. You'll freeze to death.'

'Oh . . . yes . . . I suppose I will.' His voice was dull. Were those tears below his eyes or drops of water, Christie wondered, as he got slowly to his feet and started up the beach.

They walked back to Mellon Udrigle in silence, pausing only once as the boy unhitched the Walkman from his belt, shook the water out of it and stared at it.

'That's the end of that,' he said flatly, dropping it into a peat hag.

Christie was about to remonstrate, amazed as much by the waste of something which might be mendable as by his casual littering of the place. But she changed her mind and hopped down into the hag, retrieved the Walkman and handed it back to him without saying a word. The boy merely shrugged again and fixed it back to his belt.

They arrived at the cottage and Christie was about to say goodbye when she caught something in his face, a look so abject that she felt suddenly unable to abandon him.

'Is your dad not in?' she asked.

He shook his head. 'He's gone to the pub at Aultbea to see some friends.'

'Do you want to come in, then?'

The boy looked at his feet.

'Well, do you or don't you?'

'OK.' He said it without enthusiasm.

Once inside, Christie showed him the bathroom and went to get a towel and a blanket. 'By the way, what's your name?' she asked, handing them to him through the half-open bathroom door.

'Tom,' came the reply.

'And I'm Christie. You'd better not be too long in there, I'm freezing.'

An hour later they sat in the sitting room drinking hot chocolate. Christie had drawn the curtains — it was dark now — and stoked up the coal fire which, apart from the kitchen stove, was the only other source of heating in the cottage. She was wearing a thick nightie and a dressing gown. Tom was wrapped in the blanket, his hands clasped around his mug and his skinny legs and large, pale feet stretched out towards the fire.

The front door opened and a moment later Christie's grandmother came into the room.

'Shona's had tw . . .' she began, her eyes twinkling, and then she saw Tom. 'Goodness gracious! What's this? What's been going on?'

'This is Tom, Nan,' said Christie. 'He was down at the point and he . . . had a bit of an accident.'

'So it would appear,' said her grandmother. 'What happened, Tom?'

'I fell in,' he replied sheepishly, studying his mug.

So that's it, is it? thought Christie. Just, 'I fell in.' No mention of not being able to swim, of having to be fished out . . . She caught her grandmother's eye and knew immediately that her own damp hair and warm nightclothes had told the other half of the story.

'Well, well, that was a fine thing to happen, wasn't it. It must have been terribly cold. But you're warmer now, I daresay?'

Tom nodded.

'I saw your dad's car coming back a few minutes ago. Shall I go across and tell him you're all right — he must be wondering where you are?'

'I wouldn't bother,' said Tom, still staring into his mug.

'Well, you can't go home in that blanket. I'd best go over and get some dry clothes for you.'

'OK.'

Christie's grandmother pulled on her coat and went out.

When she returned she handed Tom a jumper and a clean pair of jeans with which he disappeared into the bathroom. A few minutes later he emerged, fully dressed and carrying his damp things in a plastic bag. He poked his head into the sitting room and mumbled:

'Goodnight.'

Christie heaved a sigh of relief as the door closed behind

him. She was beginning to feel sleepy from the cocoa and the heat of the fire.

'You rescued him, didn't you?' said her grandmother as Christie kissed her goodnight.

'Yes,' Christie replied. 'But I can't think why I bothered.'

Her grandmother smiled. 'He's all right, that laddie. He just needs someone to be nice to him.'

'Well, I doubt it'll be me,' said Christie, climbing the stairs.

Chapter 4

Next morning her grandmother left early for Inverness. Christie breakfasted alone, then collected her book and went outside. It was another beautiful day.

To her surprise Neil Cameron was there, digging his garden in the sunshine. He looked up as she came out of the cottage and paused, leaning on his spade.

'Morning, Christie,' he called.

'Hello, Neil. Aren't you at work today?'

'No, it's a Forestry Commission holiday.' He grinned broadly and Christie realised he was having her on. 'Actually, the snow-cat's being overhauled and we can't get out to the new plantings without it. And what're you up to today?'

'Just going down to the beach to read.'

'You're a great one for the books, aren't you.'

Christie nodded. 'I like reading.'

'Well, don't forget to say hello to Shona and the twins on your way. They're down in the field.'

Christie crossed the road and entered the field. Shona was down in the far corner, chewing absent-mindedly while the twins guzzled their breakfast, one on either side of her, their stumpy tails vibrating with pleasure. She walked over and scratched affectionately at their mother's bony head through its coarse, black curls.

'Well done, Shona,' she said. 'Well done, old girl. Now, what are we going to call these babies of yours?'

Shona did not appear to have given the matter much thought. She rubbed her head against Christie's leg and continued chewing. The lambs, meanwhile, had emerged to see who the visitor was. One, finding itself too close to this alarming new creature, took an anxious step back, bumped into its twin and fell over.

'Laurel and Hardy, I think,' said Christie, laughing. She gave Shona a pat on the head. 'You get on with your breakfast, now.'

She climbed the far wall and dropped down to the beach. It was empty. She made for the dune again, scooped a body-hollow out of the soft, white sand and settled down.

She opened the book and began to read, but soon found that she was not taking anything in. Her mind kept returning to the various events of yesterday afternoon. She still felt uneasy about the thing that had happened at the burial ground and in trying not to think about it she found herself concentrating instead on the encounters with two men. There had been something almost as disturbing, although probably more explainable, about *that* whole episode. Why had the diver been so concerned to find her in the landrover? Was there something in there she shouldn't have seen? And his panic at the lost sheet or sheets of paper: that wasn't the reaction of someone who'd mislaid a few cage inspection reports.

Not only had she not liked him, she'd actually disbelieved almost every word he'd said, she now realised. And the man in the car — he was a bad driver and thoroughly unpleasant with it, but there was something about his association with the diver that damned him further. Maybe she'd tell Kenny about it next time she saw him. Perhaps the diver had been up to something he shouldn't have been. Perhaps they both had. Yes, she should definitely talk to Kenny . . .

Christie heard footsteps approaching across the sand and looked up. Her heart sank as she saw that it was Tom. She had hoped that after last night's drama he might have gone fishing with his father today.

'Hello,' he said, stopping in front of her.

'Hello,' she replied without enthusiasm.

Tom appeared to be having trouble with whatever it was he was going to say next. He opened his mouth, then closed it, shuffled his feet and eventually sat down on the sand in front of her, flushed with embarrassment.

'I came to say thank you,' he mumbled, avoiding her eye, '. . . for . . . you know . . . well . . . saving me yesterday.'

'It wasn't anything,' said Christie. 'I'm sure you would have done the same for me.' If you knew how to swim, she thought. 'Are you OK now?'

Tom nodded and fished in the hip pocket of his jeans, then held out his hand tentatively. 'For you.'

It was a tape, already much played, it appeared, from the condition of the plastic case. Christie took it and examined the cover, expecting it to be some current chart album. But it was not. It was The Bothy Boys, a new group from Aberdeen whose barnstorming renderings of the old folk-songs had earned them their own TV show and a series of sell-out concerts all over Scotland.

'Thank you,' she said, surprised and genuinely delighted. 'Thank you very much. Do you like this kind of stuff, then?'

'Yes. Do you?'

'I love it.'

'I thought you would.'

'Why . . . how?'

'Just guessed.' He shrugged.

'Good guess. It's what we listen to at home. My mum and dad used to play in a folk group before they got married.'

'Did they? What was it called?' For the first time since she had met him, Christie noticed a glimmer of something in Tom's eyes.

'Oh, you wouldn't have heard of it. I think they just used

to play the pubs in Inverness. Anyway, it was years ago, when they were both at teachers' training college . . .'

'That's what I'd like to do,' Tom broke in. 'Have my own folk group. I started playing guitar last year.'

'Are you any good?'

'Well . . . yeah . . . not brilliant, but I can play a few things. And my singing's not too bad.'

'Sing something now, then. Go on!' Christie was suddenly curious. Would he? Tom stared at his feet in indecision, then looked up and shook his head, flustered.

'Oh, go on. I'd like to hear you.'

'Really?'

'Yes, really!'

'What shall I sing then?'

'Oh, I dunno . . . what about 'Speed bonny boat'?'

'OK.' He cleared his throat and began:

> Speedy bonny boat
> Like a bird on the wing
> Onwards the sailors cry . . .

Somewhat to Christie's surprise his voice was a pleasant tenor. He sang clearly and in tune, the words resonating firmly across the deserted beach. She looked at him, trying to equate the strong, adult voice with the gangly, adolescent physique. They didn't really seem to fit.

> Carry the lad
> Who was born to be king
> Over the sea to Skye.

'That was good,' said Christie.

'D'you think so?' The flush was returning to his pale cheeks.

'I do. I'd like to hear you play it with your guitar. I like singing too. We could do a duet.'

He turned scarlet. 'I've . . . er . . . got it with me. It's in the cabin. Shall I get it?'

Christie nodded. Tom climbed to his feet and sprinted off across the beach, his physical awkwardness abandoned. Sand spurted at his heels.

A minute or two later he returned, panting, and sat down again. He unzipped the plastic carry-case and carefully pulled out his guitar. Its varnished surface shone in the sunlight as he placed it across his knee and began to tune it. It looked expensive, thought Christie, noticing at the same time that Tom's fingers, deftly manipulating the tuning heads, were unusually long and slender.

'Is it new?' she asked.

He nodded proudly. 'Got it for my birthday, six weeks ago. My folks gave it to me.'

'How old are you?'

'Sixteen. You?'

'Fifteen.'

'When?'

'End of January — 30th.'

'Aquarius. Bit of a dreamer?'

Christie smiled. 'Sometimes . . . maybe . . . but not always, . . . What are you, then?'

'Pisces. I'm a fish.'

'I've never met a fish that couldn't . . .' She checked herself as she realised what she was saying, but it was already too late. Tom stopped tuning the guitar and looked up at her, the hurt evident in his eyes.

'That wasn't very funny.'

'I'm sorry, I'm really sorry,' Christie stammered, aghast at her own stupidity. 'It was only a joke. I didn't mean to . . .'

Tom ignored her. Slowly and deliberately he put the instrument back in its case, then stood up.

'You shouldn't have said it.' He gave Christie a long look, bitter and reproachful. Then he turned round and walked off down the beach, his shoulders sagging.

Christie watched his retreating figure, wondering

whether to run after him and try to make amends. She was startled to find how angry she was with herself at having upset him . . .

Put-put, put-put, put-put. A boat was turning into the bay. It was a white, fibreglass dinghy, probably from the hotel at Laide, she thought. A man sat at the tiller and in the bows a small boy was hauling in a line.

The sense of *déjà vu*, when it came, was so powerful that Christie could almost feel it in her brain. She caught her breath and watched, frozen, as the little boat nosed in towards the shore, every detail brilliantly clear in the sunlight — the movement of the boy's arms, the relaxed posture of the man, leaning back in one corner of the stern. As if in slow motion, she saw his hand reach for the outboard and cut the engine.

The sudden silence galvanised her. She tore across the sand towards the cabins shouting desperately:

'Tom! Stop! Tom! The boat — something awful's going to happen!'

Tom had reached the end of the beach. As she pelted towards him he stopped and turned round, looking surprised and mildly suspicious.

'We've got to get Neil Cameron's boat out,' she gasped, tugging at his arm. 'They're going to fall in!'

At that moment the splash echoed across the bay. They turned to see the man surface and shake the water from his eyes.

Tom shrugged Christie's hand away from his arm. 'So he fell in. Big deal. It's not far to swim.'

'But it's not just him . . . there's a boy too . . . and he can't find him . . . you'll see in a minute . . .' She was almost incoherent now. 'Please, please — you don't have to believe me — just help me get the boat out.'

'You're daft,' said Tom, putting down his guitar with a look of resignation and following her to the mouth of the burn.

'Michael! MICHAEL!' The man's voice rang out, ragged with panic.

They had the boat halfway to the water when Neil Cameron came panting towards them, his face crimson.

'Well done,' he said, breathing heavily. 'There's a wee lad in there somewhere. I saw him go in from my garden. Christie, go and get some towels and blankets. You come with me, young man.' Before Tom had time to say anything Neil pushed him towards the stern, grabbed the bows himself and between them they trundled the dinghy the last few yards to the water.

Christie ran back as fast as she could to the cottage and went to the airing cupboard in the bathroom. By the time she emerged she could see that they'd got the man into Neil's boat and were circling the upturned dinghy, all three of them peering down into the water.

Christie knew that it would be clear on a day like this. They'd easily be able to see the bottom which was flat and sandy and uncluttered by rocks or weeds. All they had to do was locate the boy and dive for him — it wouldn't be difficult. She couldn't imagine why it was taking so long.

A minute passed, and another. The knot in Christie's stomach tightened as Neil's dinghy continued its circles, each one a little wider than the previous one. Then, at last, they broke off and rowed back towards the upturned hull. Now what was happening?

As they drew close the man dived into the water and swam to the boat, grasped it by the gunwales and heaved at it. The hull rocked but remained where it was. He tried again. At the third attempt the gunwales lifted clear of the water, teetered and then swung over as the boat righted itself. A triumphant cheer floated across the bay as a second head popped up beside it. Then Neil and Tom were reaching down to help them aboard.

Christie returned to the beach clutching an armful of towels and blankets. She handed a towel to the man, who nodded gratefully and began to undress. The boy, who looked about five or six, was sitting helplessly on the sand as Neil and Tom peeled off his sodden shirt and trousers. His skin was bluish-white, his teeth chattered and he was staring vacantly into the middle-distance, lost in shock. As soon as he was down to his underpants Christie began to pummel him with the big, rough towel. He began to whimper.

'Lucky little beggar, aren't you,' said Neil, patting the boy on the head. 'You gave us all a hell of fright.'

'What happened?' asked Christie, still rubbing hard at the goose-pimply flesh. A little colour was starting to flow back.

'He was hanging on to one of the thwarts — just hanging there under the hull with his head in an air pocket. No wonder we couldn't see him!' Neil began to laugh. 'Just hanging there — like a wee monkey!' He coughed and dabbed at one eye.

A moment later Tom joined in. The boy stopped whimpering as a broad grin spread across his father's face and then they too were laughing.

'A wee drowned monkey!' spluttered Neil, his chest heaving.

'Monkey, monkey!' cried the boy, hopping up and down.

Christie wanted to laugh too but found she couldn't. There was some new and entirely unfamiliar sensation stopping her. It was the same thing that was beginning to make her shake, from deep inside. For a moment she tried to identify it, but could not.

Then it came to her.

She was afraid.

Afraid of herself.

'You take over,' she said hoarsely, thrusting the towel at Tom.

She turned tail and fled back to the cottage.

The dark shape within her was gaining definition as she ran, becoming more dragon-like, and now it was fully awake.

Chapter 5

Christie paced the kitchen as gusts of panic swept through her, quickening her heartbeat and weakening her knees. She could feel it, almost see it, down in its shadowy lair, dilating its nostrils and snorting a misty, shapeless fear which swirled through her chest, down to her belly and up into her head.

'Stop it! STOP IT!' she muttered through clenched teeth. She slammed her fist on the table, close to tears.

The sound of her own voice and the sudden sharp pain in her hand were strangely reassuring. She sensed the panic starting to recede and sat down, feeling light-headed and drained.

There was no pretending now. She had seen something before it had happened. Did that make her a freak? Was it some kind of madness? What if it happened again? What if she saw something really terrible and she had to tell people and they wouldn't believe her? There was some kind of responsibility attached to all this, she realised vaguely, but quite what for, or to whom, she had no idea.

Where did this . . . this knowledge come from? Was it inside her, or was it blown into her on the wind? Whichever it was, it seemed that it was quite beyond her control —

and that was where her fear lay . . .

She sat up, trembling, and looked around for something to distract her. Maybe a hot drink would help. She went to put the kettle on and heard a knock at the door.

It was Tom with the wet towels.

'Mr Cameron said I was to bring these back. He's taken the two of them over to the hotel and he says he'll bring the blankets later.'

Although her mind was elsewhere, Christie could not help registering the flatness in his voice, the coldness in his eyes.

'Oh . . . fine . . . I mean . . . thanks,' she heard herself say.

'Well, what shall I do with them?' He was still holding them, looking at her expectantly.

She forced herself to concentrate. 'Sorry . . . here . . .' she held out her hand, 'give them to me.'

He passed them to her. Now he was staring at her, hard. 'You look as if . . .'

'Look, Tom,' she interrupted quickly, 'I feel terrible about what I said earlier on. I honestly didn't mean to hurt you. It was a stupid thing to say and I'm sorry. And I'd still like to hear you play.'

'Oh yeah?'

'I mean it, really. What about if I come over to the cabin later, when my nan's back. Could I . . . ?'

Tom continued to stare at her, then nodded. 'OK — then you can tell me what was going on back there.' He waved over his shoulder towards the beach. 'Deal?'

'Deal,' said Christie, relieved.

'See you later, then.' He turned and walked off.

'See you later,' she called after him and went back into the kitchen where she made herself a cup of tea with three teaspoonfuls of sugar and sat down again.

The hot, sweet drink was comforting, but her hands still shook a little as she held the mug and she was aware that the panic was wriggling beyond the thin veil of self-control with which she kept it at bay. She needed to get out into the fresh air, she realised, gulping down the rest of the tea.

The wind had changed while she had been indoors. She noticed it immediately. The gentle south-westerly breeze had been replaced by a stiff north-easterly which was bringing with it a heavy bank of pale grey cloud, rolling in across Caithness, Sutherland and down to Wester Ross. Although the sun still shone over Mellon Udrigle, the tops of the far hills were vanishing one by one as the cloud drew closer. The air was a good deal colder and out in Gruinard Bay the water had already grown dull and choppy.

She shivered and struck out at a brisk pace, heading across the peninsula with no particular direction in mind.

After ten minutes she crested a low hill and paused, looking down onto one of the lochans that studded the landscape like small, irregular mirrors. For some reason she found herself thinking of water-kelpies, the legendary monsters that lived in West Highland lochs and clambered out to drag hapless passers-by back into their weedy depths.

She loved the old tales and superstitions, but today the thought increased her unease. A long shadow slid across the lochan and she turned hastily away.

As she walked on, her thoughts turned again to Columba and *The Druid Saint*. Perhaps she would find answers there. She turned back towards Mellon Udrigle and broke into a trot.

Reaching the cottage she went straight up to her bedroom where she stretched out on the bed and opened the book at the marker. She read fast, skipping the descriptive parts, alert for references to his abilities as a seer.

The second half of the book was full of them: visions of crimes, battles, successes, tragedies, trivial domestic incidents, major foreign events, even a volcanic eruption; visions also of many deaths including, eventually, his own. But the more Christie read the more confused she became.

The gift came from God, Columba believed, naturally. But how he was supposed to use it, or why he had been singled out for it, Columba, or more probably the author, did not even speculate. *In time he grew accustomed* . . . That was the full extent of the author's analysis. Meanwhile the visions continued and, if he could, Columba simply passed them on to whoever they concerned, no matter how much misfortune they foretold. Imagine telling someone you'd seen them dead or dying, thought Christie.

The only small comfort the book offered was the idea that as long as you left the visions to occur spontaneously you were playing within the rules. What was not acceptable was willing them to come and making a career out of them. Christie had no intention of doing that. She hoped fervently that she would never have another.

'Christie! Are you there?' It was her grandmother. She glanced at her watch. Three-thirty. She was back early.

'I'm upstairs. Down in a minute,' she called. She got off the bed and ran a brush through her hair, then went downstairs.

Her grandmother was spreading out her shopping on the kitchen table. She looked up as Christie came in, and frowned.

'You look pale. Are you not well?'

'I'm fine, Nan.' Christie forced a weak smile, wishing again that her grandmother wasn't quite so observant. 'Did you have a good time in Inverness?'

'Yes, thanks. Here, help me put these things away, would you.'

Christie gathered tins and packets from the table and went to the cupboard, but her hands had started to tremble again and before she could get them onto the shelf she lost her grip and dropped the whole lot. Close to tears, she watched a tin of peaches roll under the dresser.

'Christie! What *is* it, dear?'

Now the fear and confusion was welling up again and Christie knew that she wouldn't have been able to answer even if she'd wanted to. She shook her head and ran from the room. She went upstairs to her bedroom, threw herself on the bed and buried her face in the pillow. The tears came.

Some time later the door opened and her grandmother came in. 'I've brought you a cup of tea,' she said.

Christie sat up and sniffed. 'Thank you.' She took the cup as her grandmother sat down on the bed. Her old cardigan had a comforting, familiar smell of sheep-feed.

'Are you feeling better now?'

'Yes . . . yes, I am.'

'Would you like to talk?'

Christie shook her head. She couldn't . . .

'It helps sometimes. And there's nothing so bad you can't tell me.'

Christie shook her head again.

'Oh well, just so long as you're OK. Drink your tea now and then maybe we'll go for a walk.' She rose and made her way across the room. Suddenly Christie didn't want to be left alone.

'Nan, I . . . I don't think you'll believe me.'

Her grandmother paused with her hand on the door handle. She turned round and smiled gently. 'Try me.'

Reluctantly, Christie told her, starting at the burial ground and ending on the beach with the rescued man and boy. Her grandmother listened in silence, nodding from time to time and smiling encouragingly when Christie faltered.

At length she leaned across the bed and clasped her grand-daughter's hands. 'It does happen, you know,' she said gently. 'You're not the only one . . .' She paused, then: 'It's called the second sight.'

'That sounds like a disease,' said Christie wretchedly. 'I'm frightened, Nan.'

'And why are you frightened?'

'Because I don't know where it comes from . . . what else I might see . . . what I'm supposed to do with it . . . and because . . . well . . . it makes me different and I don't want to be different. Not this way, at least . . .'

Her grandmother thought for a moment.

'Would you think you were different if you were an

especially good pianist, or maybe a talented athlete?'

'No . . . well . . . ye-es . . . but not in the same way.'

'Ahh, Christie, but it is the same really. It's a special gift. You see, we all have a little bit of music in us, we can all run or jump a wee bit and I believe we all have a little of the sight too. Sometimes . . . let's see . . . we know we're going to get a letter or a phone call from someone before it comes.'

Christie nodded.

'But some people have that extra bit more music, or physical power. They didn't choose it — it was given to them, maybe by God. And some other people, like you, can see things that much more clearly. Quite a lot of people in the West Highlands can — I don't know why — it seems they've done it here for centuries.'

'I know. I've been reading about St Columba.'

'Oh, that old book! It's not very good, is it?'

'Well . . . it didn't seem to tell me very much.'

'But he is sometimes called The Father of Second Sight. And he brought Christianity to Scotland and they made him a saint. Now would they have done that if they'd thought his gift was a terrible thing?'

'I suppose not.'

'No, they would not. And that reminds me, did you ever know he was supposed to have founded a little church where the burial ground is now?'

Christie paused as something, she wasn't quite sure what, seemed to drop into place in her mind. 'No, I didn't. But maybe that's got something to do with it all — my being there when I had the . . . the vision. And you know, Nan, I didn't really choose the book, it chose me.'

'Maybe so, maybe so. Perhaps you were preparing yourself without realising it.' Her grandmother looked at her directly. 'Christie, dear, I don't pretend to understand these things, I don't think anybody does. But that doesn't stop me believing them. And I do believe that what you've just seen you saw with the second sight. It may be the only time it will ever happen to you . . .'

'But if it isn't — that's what scares me, Nan. What if it does happen again and I see something dreadful?'

Her grandmother studied the back of her hands.

'I don't think you can worry for that,' she said at length. 'It would be like living in fear of being run over the whole time, or getting cancer.'

'Some people do!'

'I know, and their lives are not good. No, Christie, you're a happy girl, an intelligent girl — far too sensible to let something like this interfere with the joy of your young life. You cannot fear something that may never happen. And if it does happen, then I don't doubt you'll find the way of dealing with it. Columba did!'

'D'you really think so?'

'I do. We all discover parts of ourselves which take more getting used to than others, and we all find our own manner of coping with them.'

'Even if it's . . .' Christie hesitated, feeling at the same time foolish and slightly afraid of uttering the words, '. . . even if it's a dragon?' She saw her grandmother's incomprehending look and added quickly: 'That's what it feels like to me — a dragon.'

'A dragon, does it?' She paused, then asked: 'And what do dragons usually do?'

Christie reflected for a moment before replying: 'They guard hidden treasure.'

Her grandmother nodded, smiling. 'And whose treasure would this one be guarding, then?'

'Mine, I suppose,' said Christie, thoughtfully.

'Don't be late now!' They had finished eating and Christie was putting on her coat to go over to the cabin.

'Nan! I'm fifteen.' She pulled a face.

'Yes, dear. But I'd rather you were back by ten-thirty. It is what . . .'

'. . . Mum and Dad said. I know. I'll be back.'

She left the cottage and made her way down to the beach.

The cloud had closed right in now and the light was failing. A strong, cold wind whipped up the little bay and blew a spray of sand off the dune-crests. She wondered what she was going to say to Tom.

Outside the cabin two cars were parked, one a dark green Range Rover and the other a dirty grey estate car which looked not unlike the one that had nearly run her over the day before.

She knocked, hearing voices and the clink of glasses. A moment later the door was opened by a large sandy-haired man with pale blue eyes set in a square, weathered face. He looked at her quizzically and Christie found herself noticing the size of his neck, which seemed to drop straight from his ears and spread out beneath the patterned fisherman's sweater to his collar-bones.

'Yes?' he said.

'Is Tom in?' she asked hesitantly.

'Yes, he is. Are you Christie?'

She nodded.

'I'm Bill Davidson. Tom's father.' He grasped her hand and shook it. 'Come in, come in.' He smiled an easy, practised smile in which the pale blue eyes did not participate.

He ushered her into the pine-furnished living room. A log fire crackled in the stone fireplace and in the centre of the room stood a round dining table strewn with papers, a bottle of whisky and three tumblers. Two men sat with their backs to the door. As they turned round she was startled to see that it was the maniac driver and the diver.

'Hello,' she said, awkwardly.

'So you know each other already?' The signs of recognition had not escaped Bill Davidson's attention.

'Well . . . sort of,' said Christie.

'Yesterday, after I'd dropped off the proofs,' said the older man casually. He sniffed and fixed her with a disapproving eye.

42

The diver gave a short, nervous laugh. 'And at *Loch na Bei* . . .'

'Did you find your papers, then?' Christie interrupted. She was pleased to see that the question disconcerted him.

'What papers were those, Dougal?' asked the driver sharply.

'Oh, just some cage inspection reports that blew away in the wind. Yes, I found them, thanks.' He lowered his eyes and fiddled with the bandage at his wrist.

'Well, well.' said Bill Davidson. 'It is a small world. Christie — I don't know your last name . . .'

'McKenzie.'

'. . . Christie McKenzie, this is Bertie Ross,' he indicated the driver, 'and Dougal Mackay,' the diver. 'Christie fished my half-witted son out of the sea last night.'

'Must've been crazy,' muttered Mackay without looking up. 'At this time of year . . . and no wet-suit.'

'She had no choice,' said Tom's father, putting his arm around Christie's shoulder. 'Silly little bugger can't swim. It was lucky she was there. At least I suppose it was . . .' The three men laughed. Christie blushed uncomfortably.

'Anyway, where's he gone? He was here a moment ago. Skulking in his bedroom again I expect. Tom! TOM! Your rescuer's here!'

A door opened at the far end of the living room and Tom poked his head out. He avoided his father's eye as he looked across the room and said to Christie:

'Oh, it's you. Hello.' He disappeared back into the room leaving the door ajar. Christie presumed he meant her to join him so she made for the door. Passing the table she glanced casually at the papers which covered its surface. In the centre was what looked like a printer's proof of the front cover of some kind of brochure. it featured a map of Scotland, coloured diagonally with alternating green and gold stripes. Above the map, partially obscured by another sheet of paper, were the words:

ALBA N . . .
A New Future For . . .

She crossed the room and entered Tom's. It was as she had expected. Clothes spilled from an open suitcase. The bed was unmade. Two empty coke cans and a pile of dog-eared thrillers cluttered the bedside table. The dressing table was almost invisible under an enormous portable stereo and more tapes than Christie had ever seen outside a record shop. By the door sat the plastic bag with his damp things still in it.

'I didn't think you'd come,' he said. He looked hunched and awkward again.

'Well I did,' she replied, stepping over the guitar case and sitting down on the bed. 'We made a deal, didn't we?'

He nodded. 'Do you want a drink? There's coke, lemonade . . .'

'Coke would be fine.'

He left the room and returned with two cans, cleared a space on the floor and sat down. He studied his shoes as they drank in silence. Christie began to wish she hadn't come.

'Are they friends of your dad's?' she asked, pointing at the sitting room.

Tom shrugged. 'Not really. I think they work for him. They both seem a bit shifty to me. Give me the creeps.'

'Me too,' said Christie, relieved to hear it. 'One of them nearly ran me over yesterday. Anyway, what does he do, your dad?'

'He has raspberry farms at Blairgowrie, but he doesn't spend much time on them now. He's got managers. I think he's made stacks of money. He's away a lot of the time.'

'Doing what? Fishing?'

'No, politics. He's started some new kind of party . . . look, he's not that interesting. Do we have to talk about him?'

'Sorry.'

The silence returned.

'What about your mum, then,' Christie asked at length. 'D'you get on with her?'

'Oh yeah, she's great. We have a good laugh. He gives her a bit of a hard time sometimes. But she's no fool, my mum. She stands up to him — and he takes it from her . . .'

'But no one else?'

'Something like that,' Tom mumbled.

'So what do you get up to at home?' Christie asked, changing the subject.

'Oh, this and that. Help Mum with odds and ends, try and stay out of my dad's way and do my own thing. See my friends. Go to the movies. Play music.'

Christie hesitated, then said: 'What about our deal, then? Will you play something now?'

'OK.' Tom pulled the guitar out of its case and checked the tuning. Then he began to play:

> Ye hielands and ye lawlands
> Oh, whar hae ye been
> They have slain the Earl o'Moray
> And laid him on the green . . .

As he played, the music quickly absorbed him. His shoulders straightened and his voice firmed. Christie knew the song well and loved the slow minor chords, the haunting sadness of the story it told. The Bonnie Earl of Moray had been handsome, talented and the favourite of the wife of James VI. In a fit of jealousy the king had ordered the Earl of Huntly to 'bring him in' on a charge of aiding the lawless Earl of Bothwell. But Huntly had exceeded his authority and had cruelly murdered the unsuspecting Moray whose wife waited patiently for him on the battlements of their castle:

> Lang may his ladye
> Look frae the Castle Doune
> Ere she sees the Earl o'Moray
> Come soundin' through the toun

Christie found herself joining in the chorus, singing a simple harmony to Tom's plaintive melody. Tom looked up with the flicker of a smile and began the second verse.

Oh, wae betide ye, Huntly . . .

The bedroom door opened and Tom's father peered in.

'Turn it down a bit, would you. We're doing some work out here.' The door closed again.

Tom shook his head angrily and laid down the guitar.

'I don't understand him. He gives me a guitar for my birthday but he doesn't like it when I play.'

'But you're good. He ought to be proud of you.'

'Well, he has a funny way of showing it. Anyway, that's my bit done . . .' He closed the subject and looked at Christie expectantly.

'So what can I tell you?' She tried to sound nonchalant but she could feel herself colouring.

'Why you ran away. And why you looked so terrible when I came up with the towels.'

'I think it was just shock really. The whole thing gave me a fright. I felt sick.'

Tom looked at her penetratingly. 'That's not it,' he said. He paused for a moment, searching his memory. ' "They're going to fall in." You said it before they did.'

'It was just . . . the way he was standing up. I guessed. You'd have seen it too, it was obvious. They didn't know about boats.'

Tom shook his head, impatient. 'No, no. You had this really strange look on your face. C'mon, tell me!'

Christie drew breath, realising that he wasn't going to let her get away with it: 'OK. I knew it was going to happen before it did.'

'How?'

'I saw it happening yesterday, when I was up at the burial ground.'

'What?' Disbelief was beginning to spread across Tom's face. 'Like some kind of fortune teller?'

46

'I suppose so.'

He shook his head and began to laugh. 'You're weird. Really weird. You don't expect me to believe that, do you?'

'Believe what you like,' said Christie angrily. 'That's what happened, and I don't tell lies.'

She glanced pointedly at her watch and got to her feet. 'Anyway, I've got to go home now,' she said.

'Suit yourself,' Tom muttered as she closed the door behind her.

She walked swiftly through the living room, nodding goodnight to the three men as she passed. Then she left the cabin and made her way back across the darkened beach to the cottage.

It had begun to sleet.

Chapter 6

Christie woke up with the wind still gusting strongly, rattling the old window frames in the bedroom. The sky was overcast and she could see a dull whiteness covering the far hillsides.

'Woollies on today!' said her grandmother cheerfully as Christie came into the kitchen. 'Winter's back, it seems.' She was wearing a second cardigan over the top of her usual one.

Christie shivered and stood close to the stove. A draught was whistling in under the back door.

'We'll have a hot breakfast this morning. Porridge or bacon and eggs, or both?'

'Just porridge, thanks, Nan.'

'If it keeps up like this you'll be glad to be home. It'll be a good deal warmer down there.'

Christie thought of the solid stone headmaster's house which was set back from Mallaig harbour on the hillside, with its view across the water to the southern tip of Skye. It probably would be warmer at home — it was a good seventy miles south as the crow flies, three times that distance by road. And it was much more sheltered. Here there was literally nothing between Gruinard Bay and the North Pole.

But she wasn't ready for the holidays to end yet.

'Maybe,' she said. 'But I'm fine here.'

When the porridge came, Christie took a few spoonfuls and pushed it aside.

Her grandmother looked at her askance. 'What's happened to the appetite? You're not still thinking, are you?'

'No, no. I felt better after we talked yesterday. It's not that.'

'What is it then?'

Christie shrugged. 'I'm not really sure. I just feel restless.' She couldn't bring herself to say that she was upset that Tom hadn't believed her; and it was a bit more complicated than that, anyway. She suspected he had believed her but didn't dare admit it.

'Well now, what are you going to do today?'

'I haven't thought yet.'

'How about taking your bike up to Janet's. There are some provisions I forgot to get in Inverness. It'll blow the cobwebs away.'

The wind was at her back as Christie pedalled away from Mellon Udrigle. She could taste the salt on it as it whipped round the sides of her hood and brought the blood rushing to her cheeks.

There was a thrilling bleakness in the land on a day like today. With the cloud swirling low over her head, the gale roaring down from Scandinavia and the emptiness around her, she felt she was pitting herself against nature. And there was always the safety of a warm cottage to retreat to.

As she drew level with *Loch na Beiste* she found herself thinking again about Dougal Mackay, the diver. What on earth did he have in common with Tom's father? Or the maniac driver, come to that — Bertie Ross or whatever-his-name-was?

They seemed such unlikely companions for Bill Davidson who was evidently a successful businessman and a personality to be reckoned with — it was apparent in his build and Christie had sensed it in his voice and look, too. She had got the impression from Tom that he was used to getting his own way, and was probably not too bothered how he went about it. Dougal Mackay, by contrast, was an ordinary local from Gairloch with an average sort of job. Rude, yes. Shifty, too. But there seemed nothing special about him and as for Bertie, heaven knew where he fitted in. Even his name was all wrong.

Bertie — that was that jolly upper class twit with a monocle in the book her father was always going on about. The one with the butler. Bertie Woofter . . . no, Wooster. This one, Ross, was about as jolly as an undertaker. Bertie. What a stupid name. What was it short for? Bertrand . . . ? No. Albert . . . Yes, that was more likely. He could just about be an Albert. Albert Ross. Wait a minute . . . Albertross! Christie chuckled to herself. Albatross . . . his parents couldn't really have done that to him. But with his sour expression and his beak of a nose, it was just what he looked like.

Thinking of Alba though, that's what had been on the brochure. Alba something . . . It was the old name given by the Romans to the untamed wilderness north of Hadrian's Wall. She knew that from school, but where had she heard of 'Alba' recently? An image of the blackened, twisted wreckage of the Invercarron paper mill came immediately to mind. PAA . . . what did that stand for again? People's Army of Alba. Couldn't be anything to do with that, surely . . . ? Whatever else Tom's father might be, she was certain he was not a terrorist . . .

'Just terrible weather for the lambing. Couldn't be worse. Couldn't be worse.'

A small wiry man wearing mud-spattered waterproof trousers and cape stood at the post office counter, shaking his head. His hands were spread in front of him, red with cold. Behind the counter Janet Bain crossed her arms and nodded sympathetically, a tall, thin woman with a helmet of permed white hair and rather too much powder on her cheeks which glistened faintly under the strip light.

'And the forecast's for more snow. The weather's gone mad, you know, Euan.'

'Aye, it has that, Janet.' He shook his head again. 'Well, I'd best be off now. Cheerio.' He made for the door, nodding to Christie as he passed.

'Hello, Christie,' said Janet, smiling pleasantly. 'And what will it be today?'

'I've to get some things for Nan, please.' she replied, handing her list across the counter.

As Janet reached for the shelves Christie's eye fell on *The Ullapool Courier*, a stack of which lay folded on the counter. Halfway down the front page, just above the crease, was a photograph of a vaguely familiar face. She lifted the top copy and spread it out. It was Bill Davidson, smiling to the photographer on the steps of what looked like a village hall. Over his shoulder peered the lugubrious face of the albatross.

Mr Bill Davidson and Mr Albert Ross after the meeting in Gairloch, ran the caption. So she'd been right about the name, thought Christie, scanning the headline that ran below it: *Alba Nova chief states aims*. She began to read the article:

Mr Bill Davidson, chairman of Davidson Holdings, the Perthshire agricultural group, last week took time off from a fishing holiday to talk to Gairloch residents about the aims of the new nationalist political movement, Alba Nova, of which he is one of the founding members . . .

'Have you met him yet? He's staying in one of the cabins, you know.' Janet was leaning over the counter, looking at the photograph upside down. Her eyes glinted at the prospect of further information.

'Yes, last night,' Christie replied. She was not in the mood to feed Janet's curiosity and changed the subject. 'What is this Alba Nova, Janet?' she asked.

'Alba Nova — New Scotland. It's some sort of breakaway group from the Scottish Nationalists, I think. I know they're hot on ecology and they want their own government in Edinburgh. I can't see any difference between them and the Scot Nats, to be honest, except that they seem to be at each other's throats all the time. Anyway, they're all daft as far as I'm concerned. This country could never run itself. Where's the money going to come from? That's what I'd like to know.'

'But they're not . . . terrorists, are they? asked Christie, hesitantly. She always felt unsure of herself when it came to politics.

Janet laughed. 'Heavens to goddness, no! That's those what-d'you-call-ems, the ones that blew up the paper mill at Invercarron . . .'

'People's Army of Alba.'

'That's it. They're a right wild bunch, that lot. No, no. It's not them. Mind you, Mr Davidson'll have to change his outfit's name if those idiots keep blowing things up. People might start confusing them.'

Christie paused, then asked: 'And what's Ber . . . Mr Ross got to do with it? He was at the cabin last night too, with another man. Dougal Mackay he was called, a diver with Gairloch Salmon. I saw him at the cage the day before yesterday.'

'Och, just a couple of local layabouts looking for something to get involved in,' said Janet dismissively. 'Bertie Ross has a quarry up Loch Maree way and he's conned Mr Davidson into making him the local secretary of Alba Nova. Dougal Mackay, well you know about him, he's the treasurer — and that's a right laugh. Never has any money of his own. Always on the scrounge. If I were Mr Davidson I'd be on the lookout for that one.'

'How d'you mean — on the lookout?'

'Well, let's just say he . . . doesn't have the greatest reputation in the area.' Janet handed a carrier bag over the counter and helped Christie fill it with the provisions.

'Will we put that on your nan's bill, then?'

Christie nodded. 'Thanks, Janet.' She turned to go.

'By the way, what's that young Davidson lad like? It seemed to me his dad's pretty hard on him.'

'Oh, he's OK,' said Christie non-committally. 'Cheerio.'

Christie took the gale full in her face as she rode home. On the flat it was like pedalling up a stiff hill; where the road climbed she simply dismounted and wheeled the bike beside her. It was only three miles from Laide to Mellon Udrigle but right now it felt like ten.

When she reached the loch she saw that where the landrover had been parked two days ago there was now a shabby blue Cortina. She dismounted and walked down towards the water. Someone was in the boat, bent over, tinkering. He straightened as she stepped onto the jetty and the wind caught a mane of white hair.

'Hello, Kenny,' she said.

'Well, if it isn't my favourite girl-friend! Hello, Christie.' He stood up, beaming, and climbed onto the jetty. 'Cup of tea? Cucumber sandwich? Slice of cake?'

Christie laughed. It had become a standing joke. 'Yes, please! I'm frozen.'

They climbed into the car and closed the doors. Kenny poured strong brown tea from the thermos and handed her the plastic mug for the first swig.

'How d'you like my Roller?' he asked with a grin, waving at the scuffed upholstery and dusty dashboard of the car.

'Great!' said Christie, passing the mug back to him. The tea was scalding and contained at least half a pound of sugar.

'Makes a change from the landrover, anyway. I've had to lend it to Dougal Mackay, one of the divers, while his is fixed.'

'I know. I saw him here the day before yesterday.'

'Oh?' Kenny looked puzzled. 'What was he doing?'

'Diving. Cage inspection, he said.'

'Hmmm . . . that's odd. He was only here last week. The inspections are monthly.'

'And he was diving alone.'

Kenny scratched the white stubble on his chin. 'He shouldn't have been doing that. They're pretty strict about it, and quite rightly.'

'I know,' said Christie. 'I thought that too. What could he have been up to, d'you think?'

'Och, he probably left something last time and came back for it.'

'You don't think he was doing something he shouldn't? He wasn't exactly pleased to see me.'

Kenny laughed. 'No, I doubt it! He's a bit of a rascal all right, that Dougal. But he'd not get up to much in *Loch na Beiste*. I expect I'll find out what it was when I get the landrover back from him.'

Kenny was far too good-natured to be suspicious, she thought, letting the subject drop. They chatted on for another five minutes, until the mug was empty. Christie felt the warmth radiating from her stomach. Her cheeks were beginning to glow and she didn't relish the prospect of the final mile.

'Back to work, then,' said Kenny, screwing the cap back on the thermos.

'Yes, I'd better get home,' said Christie reluctantly. 'Nan'll be wondering whether I've been blown off the bike. Thanks for the tea.'

'Any time. Tulloch's teashop's always open!' He climbed out of the car, gave her a cheery wave and walked off down the jetty.

The wind seemed to have grown even stronger now and Christie made no attempt to ride the bike. Walking slowly along with her head lowered against the gale, she was halfway up the hill beyond the loch when a movement caught her eye at the roadside. It was two sheets of paper, flapping against a small boulder beneath which they had been blown and were now wedged.

She bent down and picked them up. They were stapled together and she saw immediately that the top sheet was a Gairloch Salmon cage inspection report form. She flipped it over to see a diagram showing a series of rectangles and circles joined by parallel lines with some kind of measurements marked beside them. It was probably this that Mackay had been looking for. So why had he lied last night about finding them all. What *was* going on?

She propped the bike at the roadside and walked across the heather to a large boulder where she squatted down out of the wind and looked more closely at the papers. The diagram made no sense but the simple, hand-drawn map on the reverse of the second sheet was more recognisable. It showed a wood (Christmas trees) on a hillside (humpy skyline) across which ran a road (dotted line down the middle) above a stretch of shore (wiggly waves) and a large jetty (a table with its legs in the water). By the wood were four rectangles and just below the road, a series of circles. Dotted lines ran from the rectangles to the circles and on down to the jetty. Three red crosses had been marked, one at the rectangles, one at the circles and one at the jetty.

It corresponded exactly to the diagram, she realised, undoing the staple and holding them up side by side. But what was it? Something to do with a salmon farm maybe, or a hydro-electric station? As she stared at it she began to sense that it was something with which she was familiar. She closed her eyes and eventually it came. It was the NATO fuel depot at Aultbea, five miles away.

Christie knew it well. It had been built during the last war to fuel the North Atlantic convoys at their assembly point in the deep waters of Loch Ewe. As you drove from Aultbea to Gairloch you passed beneath the tanks which poked out from the corner of the wood like the grass-covered tiers of some huge Aztec temple. Underground pipes ran down to the circular mounds of the pumping and valve stations at the roadside and then on down to the jetty with its battery of spotlights on a gantry overlooking the water. It was unmistakeable. But why did Dougal Mackay need a map of it? And what did the red crosses indicate?

Wait a minute, though. Hadn't Neil said something about security cuts and the depot being a sitting duck? He'd only been joking at the time, but what if he was right nonetheless and this was some kind of sabotage plan? Could Mackay really be with the PAA? Surely not. Much as she disliked and mistrusted him it seemed too far-fetched, too much like the plot of a movie.

All the same, the whole thing made her feel distinctly uneasy; and it was beginning to set her imagination a-whirr. She shivered, then quickly reassured herself: no, it was nothing to do with . . . the *thing* that had happened. It was just instinct.

She stuck the papers in her pocket and walked back to the road, wondering what she ought to do. She wheeled the bike over the hill and down towards Mellon Udrigle. At the turn-off to the cabins she stopped for a moment, deliberating, then left the road and set off along the track.

Ahead of her the tips of the fir trees bent low before the gale. The bay was now virtually unrecognisable as the scene of yesterday morning's rescue: the still blue water had turned milky green, churning with sand as short, powerful breakers piled in one after the other. The beach looked grey and the sandstone promontories glistened darkly with spray.

The cabin was locked. Christie walked out towards the burial ground, scanning the shore on either side of the headland. Tom was not there either. Damn it! He must have gone with his dad today.

She had begun to make her way back to the road when an oilskin-clad figure turned onto the track, head bowed against the wind. Christie walked towards it.

'I was looking for you,' she said.

Tom merely grunted, as if the effort of speech was too much.

'You look completely done in. Where've you been?'

'To the river with my dad.'

'Where's he, then?'

'Still there.'

'You mean you walked back? But it's miles . . .'

'I know.'

They had reached the cabin now. Tom fished for a key, unlocked the door and walked inside, peeling off his outer layer as he went. Christie stepped over the discarded oilskins and followed him into the sitting room as he slumped into an armchair without bothering to remove his boots. His face was pinched and Christie thought he looked close to tears.

'What happened?'

'We had a row. He shouted at me because I wasn't casting properly. The fly kept getting caught in the heather.' He paused, then added savagely: 'It's impossible in this wind!'

Christie pictured the exchange that had taken place on the wind-lashed riverbank: Bill Davidson glaring at Tom with his hard blue eyes, Tom laying down his rod, slope-shouldered and defeated. Isobel was right, no doubt about it.

'So you left him to it?'

'Yes. I walked down to the road, hitched a lift to Laide, and walked back here.'

'Why did you go in the first place?'

'I just felt I should. Keep him company . . . something like that.' He shrugged, hopelessly.

'Shall I make a hot drink? You could do with something.'

Tom nodded.

'So why were you looking for me?' he called out as she searched the cupboards of the miniscule kitchen. 'I didn't think I'd see you again . . .'

'I wanted to ask you about something,' she replied. 'D'you want tea or coffee?'

'Coffee.'

She returned with two mugs of coffee and set them down on a low table by the armchair, placing herself on the floor.

'What were you going to ask me, then?'

Christie paused with her cup halfway to her lips, uncertain how to begin.

'It's . . . to do with those two who were here last night. The diver, Mackay . . . well, I saw him the day before yesterday, down at *Loch na Beiste*. There was something funny about him . . . or rather . . . what he'd been doing.'

'How d'you mean "funny"?'

Christie recounted the detail of her meeting with Mackay, then handed Tom the diagram and the map. 'It's a map of the NATO fuel depot at Aultbea. I'm pretty sure it's what he was looking for.'

Tom looked at them. 'So?'

'So why should a diver from Gairloch Salmon have a map of the fuel depot? And what was he doing at the cage if he wasn't inspecting it?'

Tom looked at her blankly. 'You tell me.'

Christie gulped. 'I know it sounds crazy, but what if he's just pretending to be involved with your dad's thing? What if he's really with that PAA — the ones that blew up the paper mill — and the fuel depot's their next target?'

'Is this another of your . . . ?' Tom began, then stopped.

Christie blushed and shook her head. 'It's just a "What If?". Neil Cameron was saying that the depot was a sitting duck . . . something about security cuts. We both thought they were a bit shifty and I wondered whether maybe you knew something more about them?'

Tom didn't seem to have heard. He was staring out of the window. 'He *was* asking a lot of questions about you,' he said without turning round.

'Who?'

'Dougal Mackay. It was him that stopped for me and gave me a lift back to Laide.'

'What sort of questions?'

'Oh — who you were . . . where you lived . . . how well you knew the area . . . how well you knew some guy called Tulloch . . . and if I thought you were bright . . .'

'What did he mean — bright?'

'Bright — intelligent, I suppose.'

'What did you say?'

'Told him you were a genius, of course.' His face was expressionless. Christie stared at him in confusion. Then one pale eyelid flickered in an almost imperceptible wink. His smile spread slowly as Christie burst out laughing.

'Look,' he said eventually, 'it's the daftest idea I've ever heard. But let's say it's true. Does that mean the other one's in it too?'

'It wouldn't surprise me,' said Christie. 'He stopped and talked with Dougal Mackay at the loch after he'd nearly run me over. They seem to know each other, and I get the feeling he's the one in charge. By the way,' she couldn't resist it, 'you know what his real name is?'

'Haven't a clue.'

'Albert Ross. Albertross. Get it?'

'Al-ba-tross,' said Tom slowly. 'Hey, that's brilliant! Albatross the boss! And he looks like one too.' He began to laugh, then a thought came. 'You know what that would make them, of course?'

'What?' Christie was grinning at the success of her own pun.

'The People's Army of Albatross.' He threw himself back in the chair and drummed his feet on the floor. 'The People's Army of Albertross!'

'And what a pair of creeps!' spluttered Christie, slopping coffee out of her mug. Tom by now was speechless, twisting in the chair with tears rolling down his face.

'Hang on a minute, though,' he said eventually. 'If it is true, that makes my dad a terrorist . . .'

Christie dabbed at her eyes and shook her head emphatically. 'I'm sure he's not. I just think he's being conned.'

Tom snorted unsympathetically. 'That's good! My dad being conned. It would be the first time!'

'D'you think we should tell him . . . show him these?' she pointed at the maps. 'Maybe I've got it all wrong about the fuel depot, but I don't trust either of them . . . I don't think they're good people for your dad to be with, for whatever reason. And Janet at the post office said something about Dougal Mackay having a bad reputation around here. If we do tell him at least he can make up his own mind.'

'No,' said Tom, serious again now. 'It's made up already. He's an idealist when it comes to politics — at least that's what my mum keeps telling him, and she should know. Idealists don't hear what they don't want to, do they? Mackay and the albatross are his yes-men. They're going to get things moving for him up here . . . he says.'

'So what should we do?'

Tom rose from the armchair and walked over to the fireplace. He picked up the poker and jabbed at a charred log. 'Forget it. Even if you're right you'd never convince him.'

'But what do *you* think, Tom? Could I be right?' The vehemence of her question startled both of them. Tom turned round, the poker hanging limp from one hand.

'I . . . don't . . . know.' He searched her face, as if the answer might be hidden there somewhere.

'What if I could prove it to you?' she asked, startled this time by the sudden strength of her own conviction. 'What if I could show you something that would *make* your dad believe it?'

Tom looked down at the poker for a moment, then lifted his head. 'That,' he said, permitting himself a half-smile, 'I would like to see!'

Chapter 7

'Is it all right if I go over to Tom's?' said Christie as she cleared away the supper things.

Her grandmother nodded and smiled. 'I was right, wasn't I?'

'About what?'

'About Tom. He's not that bad, is he?'

Christie blushed. 'Well . . . he's a good guitarist and he has a nice voice, too — the old stuff, *our* music, Nan. You'd like it.'

'Does he now? Perhaps we could have a concert one day. Well, enjoy yourself and remember, back by ten-thirty!'

'Yes, yes, Nan!'

Christie went up to her room and dressed: extra sweater, scarf, gloves and thick socks. As she was pulling on her oilskin her eye fell on *The Druid Saint* which was sitting on her bedside table. She picked it up and stuck it away out of sight at the farthest end of the bookshelf above the bed.

Then she padded downstairs, slipped past the open kitchen door, picked up her wellingtons in the hall and called ' 'Bye, Nan' as she went outside. On the doorstep she climbed into the boots, patted the oilskin pocket to make sure the torch was there and glanced at her watch. A quarter to eight. She'd agreed to meet Tom at eight o'clock behind the trees at the cabins.

The light was grey beneath low cloud. The wind had dropped a little but the sleet had started again, slapping wetly against her face. It hardly ever snowed properly down here, close by the sea, but up on the high ground, lost in thick cloud, it was probably blowing a blizzard.

She set off across the beach towards the cabins, conscious of the tightening knot in her stomach. Why was she so certain about what they were going to do? It was not as if she'd . . . seen anything. And yet, for no logical reason her conviction had grown even stronger since talking to Tom earlier on in the day. It could be nothing more than a hunch, but it was a very strong hunch . . .

The Range Rover was parked outside the cabin and the lights were on. She slipped down the side of the wooden building and made her way through to the rear of the belt of trees. A few minutes later she heard voices at the cabin door and then the rustle of low branches as Tom approached. He had a pregnant-looking bulge in his waterproof.

'Everything OK?' she asked softly.

'Yes. I told him I was going to your place. I think he was glad to have me out of the way for the evening.' He undid his oilskin and pulled on the second sweater which had been stuffed down the front.

'Have you got the gaff?'

He nodded and patted the large poacher's pocket in the lining of his coat. 'You'd better be right about this.' There was an intensity in his face that Christie had not seen before.

'Let's go,' she said.

Keeping the trees behind them, they headed back towards the mainland in a line with the road, two hundred yards to their right. Climbing the low, heathery rise which sheltered Mellon Udrigle and the bay from the south, they dropped down the other side and continued in a straight line, still keeping their distance from the road.

A pale brown bird with a beak like a long curved surgical

instrument flapped from the ground in front of them, calling plaintively into the empty moorland.

'Curlew,' said Tom.

Christie nodded. 'Are you interested in birds?'

'Not really. My dad's pretty hot on them — it's all part of his ecology bit. He used to make me learn them when I was a kid. I suppose it's stuck.'

'Some of it . . .'

'Yes, some of it.' He let slip a quick, sheepish grin.

By the time they drew level with the loch the dusk was thickening and with it the sleet. The flakes were getting larger and despite the brisk walk Christie could feel the ends of her fingers beginning to numb. They crossed the road and made their way down to the jetty. The boat was there, oars stowed under the thwarts, and there were a couple of orange life-vests lying in the bottom.

'We'd better wait till the light goes,' she said. 'Come on, we'll walk once round the loch. That should do it.'

As they walked she told Tom the story of *Loch na Beiste* — The Loch of the Beastie. It was a true story concerning a 19th century laird who had been constantly entreated by his superstitious tenants to rid them of the terrible water-kelpie which lurked in its depths. Finally giving in to them, he had set about draining the loch with a horse-driven pump, dumping fourteen barrels of quicklime into the deepest part for good measure. But after two years of pumping no lime-scoured beastie had floated to the surface and the water had only dropped six inches; for the pump, he had discovered, was just about keeping pace with the burn which fed the loch on the other side. So he had abandoned the loch to the beastie and the tenants to their superstition.

The story had appeared in *Punch* of the day. Christie's grandmother had shown her a reproduction of the article with its cartoon of the kilted laird standing at the side of the loch, a measuring stick in one hand as he tilted back his bonnet and scratched his head with the other; while out in the water a big, whiskery dripping face was chuckling at him.

'Perhaps Mackay was making friends with it,' joked Tom in an unsuccessful attempt to conceal his nervousness.

'If I was it, I'd have eaten him,' she said tersely.

The darkness was complete by the time they returned to the jetty, the sleet a vague blurring of the vision. Christie shone her torch into the boat and reached down for the life vests. She handed one to Tom and began to put the other on herself.

He looked at it for a moment and then slipped his arms through the holes. 'There's no mystery to it, you know. I just never learnt . . . at least, I tried . . . but I couldn't get the hang of it.' He did up the ties across his chest. 'You don't need to wear one for my sake.'

'I'd rather, anyway,' she replied, climbing into the boat. Tom followed and they were about to cast off when the darkness was raked by car headlights, approaching from Laide.

'Get down!' Christie whispered, laying herself flat across the thwarts. Tom followed suit as the car engine became audible. It was slowing down, turning onto the track to the jetty, its lights wavering up and down on the water as it bumped along the rough, unmetalled surface. Then the lights came to rest. Christie held her breath, her eyes fixed on the sleet-flakes driving diagonally through the yellow beam, as she waited for the sound of the engine dying, the slamming of car doors . . .

But the engine continued to idle. After a minute or so there came a wrench of gears and a whine of complaint as the car reversed back up to the road, swung round and continued in the direction of Mellon Udrigle.

'What was all that about?' asked Tom, breathing fast.

'I don't know, but we'd better get going in case they come back.' She looked at the jetty above them. They must have been just enough in its shadow not to have been seen. She let out a long breath and grasped an oar. Tom reached for the other and they made their way out into the loch.

It took them only a dozen strokes to gain the cage. They felt the boat nose against it before the aluminium frame became visible in the beams of their torches.

'OK,' said Tom clambering into the bows and grasping the frame with one hand, 'I'll pull, you do the fishing.' They extinguished their torches and Christie moved to the side nearest the hatchery, thrusting her oar down into the water little by little and tapping it against the netting sides of the cage until eventually it met with no more resistance.

'Pull away,' she said.

Slowly they worked their way round the cage, Christie feeling every inch of the side with the oar, alert for the least sensation of an obstacle. By the time they were halfway down the third side her arm was beginning to ache and her spirits to sink as the oar continued to pass unobstructed through the water. Then, within a couple of feet of their starting point, she felt the wooden shaft turn in her hand as the blade snagged on something.

'Got it!' she said triumphantly. Tom held the boat steady, a dark shadow in the bows, as she gently tilted the oar, feeling the pressure on its leading edge as it rose slowly from the vertical to the diagonal. When she was unable to lift any further she wedged the shaft under her left arm and took the gaff from Tom with her other hand. Rolling up her sleeve, she leant as far over the side as she dared and plunged her right arm into the loch, wincing at the cold, then swept the water with the fully-extended telescopic metal tube. When it too met resistance, she pulled upwards and as it broke the surface she could see, in the beam of Tom's torch, that a rope lay within the deep curve of its hooked end.

Tom scrambled aft and together they heaved at the rope until a large black waterproof diving bag tumbled over the gunwale. They tugged at the heavy-duty velcro fastenings with numbed fingers and the first flap came open. Inside it was another, then a poppered opening and finally the contents were exposed to view.

Down one side and giving the bag its weight, were a pair of long-handled, heavy-bladed bolt-cutters. Stuffed in a corner were four black, commando-style knitted balaclavas and four pairs of industrial gloves. A cheap alarm clock lay beside a clear plastic case the size of a cigarette box, containing a dozen small silver cylinders lying on a bed of foam. At the bottom, wrapped in some sort of cling-film, was a large pudding of what looked like a pale, rubbery marzipan.

'What d'you think that is?' said Christie reaching in.

'No!' Tom's hand came down heavily on her wrist and wrenched it from the bag. His voice was shaking as he said: 'I think it's some kind of explosive.' He looked up at her in the torchlight, his face solemn.

'Jesus, Christie, you were right!'

I was too, she thought, as they resealed the bag and returned it gingerly to the water.

As they turned right onto the rough road that led along the front of the little wood to the cabins, Tom stopped suddenly.

'They're here!' He pointed to where a rectangle of light from the cabin window illuminated the rear end of the dirty estate car, protruding from behind the Range Rover. 'That must have been them at the loch. Now what do we do?'

'We just go in,' said Christie. 'They don't know where we've been. We'll wait till they've gone and then talk to your dad.'

'But we're supposed to be at your place . . .'

'That's OK. We came back to listen to music. Nan doesn't have a tape deck.'

'Doesn't she really?' He sounded slightly incredulous.

'Really.'

Tom paused. 'So you haven't listened to The Bothy Boys yet?'

'No, but I'm looking forward to it when I get home!' She smiled at him in the darkness. 'Come on!'

They moved their boots, coats and extra jumpers in the porch, then entered the living room. The three men were sitting round the fire.

'We need someone really good in Stornoway,' Tom's father was saying. 'Someone who can . . .' He looked up. 'God! Here's a pair of drowned rats. Where the devil have you been?'

'Just walking back from Christie's place,' Tom mumbled. 'It's terrible out there.' Christie could feel the other two men's gaze on her. Mackay's grey-green eyes were narrow, suspicious, as they had been at the loch. The albatross peered sourly at her and fingered the end of his nose.

'We're going to listen to some music,' said Tom, his eyes fixed on a point somewhere in the middle of his father's chest.

'OK. But keep it down. See you later, Christie.' He flashed her a quick, cold smile.

'Yes, Mr Davidson.'

They went into Tom's room. Tom closed the door and slumped down on the bed.

'He's not going to believe us, you know.' The look of apathy had returned to his pale face. He turned on one side and dangled an arm to the floor, picking distractedly at the carpet.

Christie stood by the bed, studying him. None of this was really her problem. He was Tom's father and they were Tom's father's friends. There was no reason for her to get involved . . . and yet, of course, there was. People couldn't be allowed to go round blowing things up, willy-nilly. And she was beginning to feel drawn into the Davidson family by the emotions it was arousing in her: sympathy for Tom or dislike of his father, she couldn't tell which was the stronger.

'He can make life really difficult for you, can't he,' she said.

'Yes.' The word slipped out reluctantly.

'Is he like this all the time?'

Tom fidgeted on the bed. 'No . . . yes . . . oh, I dunno!'

'Why? It seems so unfair. Just because you're different, because you'd rather play the guitar than go fishing . . .'

'He's always done that,' said Tom with resignation.

'What?'

'Wanted me to be things I'm not.'

'What sort of things?'

'I suppose . . . if I played rugby and wanted to be a farmer or a businessman we might get along. And an ace blinking salmon-catcher, of course.'

'Could you be?' It was an improbable image, she had to admit.

Tom shook his head.

'So what do you do?'

'Put up with it, I suppose . . . and hope he gets off my case sooner or later.'

Christie thought. 'This would get him off your case, you know.' She pulled the plans from her pocket.

'That's his problem. How would it help me?'

'Oh, come on, you're being dense now — or maybe you like it the way it is.'

Tom's eye flashed angrily. 'That's bullshit. Of course I don't!'

'Well, you'd help yourself by helping him.' She said it with more conviction than she felt.

He looked doubtful. 'I suppose so . . . if it's true.'

'We know it's true. Who else would that stuff belong to? You saw the way they were looking at me in there. And Dougal Mackay lied about the papers.'

Tom nodded hesitantly.

'He'd *have* to be grateful, wouldn't he?'

'He might.'

'Well then, that would be a start wouldn't it?'

Some time later the sounds of movement and raised voices came from the sitting room. Farewells followed and then the closing of the front door.

'Are you ready?' said Christie.

Tom fiddled nervously with the neck of his shirt and grunted: 'Yup.'

Christie opened the door into the sitting room. Tom's father had returned to his seat by the fire and was studying a sheaf of papers.

He glanced across the room. 'I'd forgotten you two were in there,' he said. He dropped his gaze and continued reading.

Tom shuffled and cleared his throat. 'Er . . . Dad, we've . . . er . . . something to tell you.'

'Well?'

'It's . . . to do with your friends.'

'Oh?' He laid down the papers. 'What about my friends?'

The colour rushed to Tom's cheeks as he said: 'We think that Dougal Mackay is something to do with the People's Army of Alba — the terrorists that blew up the paper mill.' He added hastily: 'We don't know about the other one — Bertie.'

Bill Davidson's jaw dropped in disbelief then hoisted itself back into the beginnings of a grin which spread all the way across his square, weathered face. He tipped back his head and began to laugh.

'Dougal Mackay, a terrorist? You've been reading too many thrillers, son.' He smacked the arm of the chair. 'Mackay, a terrorist! That's great! I'll have to tell him next time I see him!'

Christie waited till his laughter subsided, then said: 'Tom hasn't been reading thrillers, Mr Davidson. I told him about it. Dougal Mackay was diving at the salmon cage at *Loch na Beiste* the day before yesterday, when he didn't need to be. He lost some papers in the wind. I found them. They're plans of the fuel depot at Aultbea. Tom and I went out to the cage earlier this evening and we found what he'd hidden there. A bag. With explosives in it. They actually stopped at the loch on the way to see you tonight. We were there and they nearly caught us.'

Bill Davidson's smile vanished. He thrust his head

forward like a bull and stared at Christie, his blue eyes unblinking. 'That, young lady, is a very dangerous allegation. If you're inventing this you could be in deep, deep trouble.'

Christie faltered under his gaze. Before she had time to recover herself Tom came to her rescue: 'She's not inventing it, Dad, and I think it's you that could be in trouble. We're telling you because we want to help.'

His father rounded on him. 'How could you possibly help me? You can't even cast a fly in a breeze!'

Tom paled again. His lower lip quivered but he managed somehow to keep control of himself. 'By telling you the truth,' he said softly, then his grasp slipped and he yelled: 'By getting you, for once in your life, to listen to something you don't want to hear!' He sat down, trembling.

Bill Davidson leant back in his armchair with a look of astonishment. He shook his head and muttered: 'By God! He means it!'

'Yes, Mr Davidson, he does. Here, you'd better have a look at these.' Christie handed him the plans, together with a list of all the things they'd seen in the diver's bag. 'Dougal Mackay doesn't trust me,' she added. 'It's written all over his face.'

He took them and spread them on his knees. Maybe it was just the effect of the firelight, but it seemed to Christie that there was the minutest softening of his features as he studied them.

'That's the fuel depot, all right,' he said at length. 'I saw it the other day on the way to Gairloch. And these crosses, I suppose they could be . . . well . . . Now, what about this 'explosive'? What did it look like?'

'Like marzipan, or maybe a very pale putty,' said Tom, leaning forward in his chair.

'And the other bits and pieces?'

'Little silver tubes, a bit bigger than the fuse in a plug, ordinary radio batteries, coils of electrical cable — and an alarm clock.'

'Hmmm . . . that's definitely the package. Plastic explosive, detonators, an ignition system and a timer. It would do the trick.' He looked at Christie, catching her quizzical gaze. 'I did my National Service in the Royal Marines,' he said, tapping the paper with his forefinger. 'This was all part of the job.' Then he turned and stared into the fire for a long time, lost in thought.

'But what makes you so sure all this stuff belongs to Mackay?' he asked at length.

'Only what I saw,' Christie replied. 'He was diving two days ago, alone, which he's not meant to do. Kenny Tulloch from Gairloch Salmon said he'd only inspected the cage last week. He seemed quite upset that I'd been sitting in his landrover. And he didn't want me to help him look for the missing papers.'

'Well, well,' he said. 'And on the basis of that you went out in this filthy weather and poked around in the loch in the dark?' There was a glimmer of appreciation in the pale blue eyes. But so far it was directed only at Christie.

'Yes, *we* did,' she said.

He paused again, then said: 'Someone's up to no good round here, that's obvious. But you haven't convinced me it's Mackay. There's nothing here that's got his name on it. The evidence is only circumstantial.'

'What about this?' Christie showed him the Gairloch Salmon logo on the back of the sheets.

'Gairloch Salmon has dozens of employees. Mackay is only one of them.' He stood up, his features setting again like granite and his eyes growing cold. 'But I suppose I could find out. If it is Mackay, God help him!'

'So what will you do?' asked Tom. 'Tell the police?'

His father spun round and glared at him. 'NO! On no account will I tell the police.' Tom shrank back in his chair. 'Nor will you — or anyone else,' he shifted his gaze to Christie, 'and that's an order!'

'What will you do then?' asked Christie meekly.

'That needn't concern you, Christie. Now, I think you'd

better get back to your grandmother's. And you're not to say a word about this to anyone, do I make myself clear?'

'Yes, Mr Davidson. Goodnight.' She made for the door. 'See you tomorrow, Tom?'

'Yes, see you tomorrow.' He got up and followed her across the room.

'Well done!' she whispered as she put on her coat. She grasped his arm and squeezed it hard, then stepped outside.

Blinking against the large wet flakes of sleet, Christie did not notice the sudden movement in the shadows to her left as a dark figure ducked away from the cabin wall and into the concealment of the trees.

Chapter 8

Christie was at *Loch na Beiste*, swimming with Kenny Tulloch who kept offering her tea from the diving tank on his back, but she couldn't hold the cup and swim at the same time. It was very frustrating.

They were going to rescue Tom who was floating quite comfortably on his back in the middle of the loch with an orange life vest round his ankles. As they got closer she could see Tom's face clearly, with its pale skin and gingery eyebrows, but then suddenly it wasn't Tom any longer; it was Dougal Mackay and he was pulling on a sleek, black diving hood which came way down over his face, covering all his features except for the eyes. Whiskers began to sprout from beneath his nose and he was a seal, gliding towards them. The eyes, though, were not the inquisitive eyes of a seal — they were the oily, menacing saucers of a great dark water-kelpie. It was beginning to rear out of the water. Kenny would save her. But Kenny was no longer there and the water-kelpie was extending its long tentacles towards her. A warm rubbery one clamped itself across her mouth and a cold hard one pressed at her temple . . .

Christie twisted in the bed and tried to shake the tentacles from her face, but she couldn't move her head. She opened her mouth to yell but all that came out was a muffled gargling noise. She opened her eyes, becoming dimly aware as she did so that someone was saying something to her:

'Get up, lassie! Get up and get dressed!' She'd heard that voice before somewhere. She sat up slowly and the hand, for that was what it was, removed itself from her mouth; but the cold thing remained pressed to her temple. 'Not a squeak, now, or else . . . !' the voice commanded.

Terrified, Christie did as she was told, climbing out of bed and crossing the room to the chair where her clothes were folded. As her eyes grew accustomed to the darkness she glanced across the room to where the albatross sat on the edge of the bed with one arm resting on his knee. In his hand was clasped a stubby little gun from whose snout protruded the mean, dark cylinder of a silencer. It was trained at her chest.

Christie dressed in trembling silence.

'Now what?' Her voice sounded as if it didn't belong to her.

The albatross gestured at the door with his gun. 'Downstairs,' he said.

Across the landing her grandmother's bedroom door was ajar, she noticed, as she walked carefully downstairs, conscious of the pressure in the small of her back.

'Put your coat and boots on,' he said as they reached the hall. Christie obeyed. 'Now, outside. And no noise!'

It was an unnecessary command. The gale had returned, howling in from the direction of Gruinard Bay and driving the sleet almost horizontally through the pitch darkness. They walked down the garden path, through the gate and turned right along the side of the field. Christie put out an arm, partly to steady herself, partly to feel her way along the wall. This couldn't be happening! But the maggot of fear in the pit of her stomach told her sharply that she'd better believe it.

At the end of the field they followed the road to the left and fifty yards further on a prod in the back told Christie to turn left again into the small space that had been cleared as a car park behind the dunes. The vague shape of a car materialised — her grandmother's.

The albatross opened the rear door and pushed Christie towards the seat. As she climbed in she noticed that the front passenger seat and driver's seat were already occupied. She winced to see her grandmother sitting stiffly in the passenger seat, staring straight ahead. Behind the wheel, half-turned with a gun trained at her grandmother's head, was a small man Christie had not seen before. She studied the shadowed profile briefly: long nose and jaw, long sloping forehead — it could well be the albatross's younger brother or son.

The albatross climbed into the back beside her and when he had closed the door behind him, grunted to the driver: 'OK.'

The driver slowly lowered his gun to his lap, then turned the ignition. The wipers sprang to life, clearing greasy blobs of sleet from the windscreen, but the lights remained off as he reversed slowly out of the car park and set off in the direction of Laide, the front wheels every so often nudging the grass verge as he guided the car uncertainly through the sleet-spattered darkness. Only when they were over the low hill to the south of the bay did he switch on the headlights.

'Where are we going?' asked Christie nervously.

'You'll find out soon enough,' said the albatross. 'Now, belt up,' he shifted the gun in his hand, 'and don't even think of trying anything.' He leaned forward and tapped Christie's grandmother on the shoulder with the tip of the silencer. 'That goes for you too.'

Christie sensed her grandmother bristling, but she remained silent.

Don't try anything. As they approached the main road and began to slow down, Christie found herself wondering whether she could try something. Once out of the car she'd be invisible within ten yards on a night like this. But a sideways glance at the albatross, alert in the corner with his gun at the ready, dissuaded her.

They turned left, heading in the opposite direction from Aultbea and Gairloch, and drove along the southern edge of Gruinard Bay for no more than a mile before pulling into a rough lay-by where two large yellow earth-moving machines sat like dripping prehistoric monsters, caught by surprise in the headlights. The driver eased the car around the back of the nearest one, out of sight from the road, and stopped. Before he extinguished the lights Christie saw that there were two other vehicles parked in front of them: a dirty grey estate car and beyond it a dark green Range Rover.

'Out!' The albatross prodded her towards the door. She climbed out, staggering slightly in the wind as she straightened up. She could hear the sea crashing onto the shore just ahead of her. Her grandmother also emerged and stood beside her. She felt for Christie's hand in the darkness and squeezed it hard.

The two men had now moved round in front of them and stood with their backs to the wind, their weapons levelled.

'You take them down to join Dougal,' said the albatross, shouting to make himself heard. 'I'll get the car up to the quarry. Come and pick me up there and we'll get back for the Range Rover. OK?'

The driver nodded. 'Let's go then?' He pointed with his gun in the general direction of the shore. Christie went first, stepping gingerly off the gravelled surface of the lay-by onto a sheep track which wound down into the darkness. She could hear the car start up again and headlights swept the air above her head as she made her way down the track.

She trod slowly and carefully, feeling her way with her feet. The sleet was now mingling with salt spray on her face and most of the time it felt as if it was only the wind that stopped her from pitching forward as the track dipped and turned. Once or twice her grandmother stumbled behind her, grasping at Christie's oilskin to keep her balance and she heard the man curse as he, in turn, stumbled against her grandmother.

A couple of minutes passed and the track began to level.

They were almost at the shore now.

'Keep left here,' the man shouted.

Christie swung left. A deep booming began to make itself heard through the gale and their destination suddenly dawned on her. They were going to the prayer-cave.

A few moments later there was a clunking under her feet as she stepped off the track and onto the pebbles of a beach. A torch-beam stabbed the darkness and a voice called out: 'Over here!'

Now, at the base of a low, dripping cliff, she could just make out the dark opening where, in the previous century, ministers of the Free Kirk had stood like crows with the wind tugging at their black garments as they led their congregations in the strange Gaelic psalms, voices raised against the pounding of the sea. Huddled on the pebbles and boulders before them had sat their flock, reduced to worshipping in the open air because the Presbyterian landlords disapproved of their new, breakaway church and would not grant them land on which to build a permanent meeting place.

Eventually, however, a church had been built and the human flock had abandoned the cave to the four-footed variety. Christie had been here several times and she knew that now it was only ever visited by the occasional tourist with a keen interest in local history.

She also knew that it was invisible from almost everywhere except directly ahead, out in Gruinard Bay: the overhang of the cliff concealed it from the road and the short, battlement-like promontories which enclosed the beach on both sides, hid it from the rest of the shore. The booming she had heard came from another cave on the far side of one of the battlements into which the sea hurled itself, reverberating like the repetitive thunder of some enormous siege-cannon.

At the cave-mouth stood Dougal Mackay, his eyes narrow under the dark hood of his oilskin. In one hand he held the torch, in the other the gun with which he now gestured at the interior of the cave.

'Inside!'

Christie stepped inside, sensing her grandmother directly behind her. She took a pace forward, the force of the wind eased at her back and total blindness descended. She stretched out her hands like a sleep-walker, remembering that the roof shelved sharply downwards towards the rear of the cave, and groped a couple of paces through the darkness, then stumbled against something soft. Hands reached up and guided her to the floor.

'It's me, Tom!' whispered the owner of the hands as she helped her grandmother down beside her.

'Tom!'

Her grandmother's breath sounded rapid and shallow. 'Are you all right, Nan?'

'Yes, I think so, dear . . . when I get my wind back.'

Slowly Christie's eyes were acclimatising to the darkness. In the cave-mouth, the wind whipping at their oilskins, Mackay and the driver were holding an inaudible conversation. Eventually the driver gave Mackay a farewell pat on the back and disappeared from view. Mackay stepped into the cave and played his torch on the occupants. Christie gasped as the beam fell on Bill Davidson who was stretched full length on the floor, a deep gash at his forehead. He appeared to be unconscious.

'What happened . . . ?' she began to ask Tom, but at that moment there was a movement in the darkness behind her. Mackay hurriedly raised his torch and Christie turned round to see a ewe clambering to her feet at the very back of the cave. From her hindquarters dangled a dark rope of placenta and at her feet lay a small damp parcel which emitted the tiniest bleat as its mother moved forward to place her body protectively in front of it. The lamb bleated again, its cry faint and tinny against the background noise of the wind and sea, like some electronic toy whose batteries were running down.

The torch beam swung away, returning mother and

infant to the darkness as Christie's grandmother rose unsteadily to her feet and addressed herself to Mackay:

'I don't know who you are or what you're up to, but I should say you've got some explaining to do — dragging us from our beds in the middle of the night . . . waving guns around . . . and what the devil have you done to that poor man?'

As if on cue, Bill Davidson groaned and struggled to sit up. He clasped one hand to his head and fell back again. Mackay lifted his gun a couple of inches.

'Why don't you just put that thing away!' continued Christie's grandmother. 'You should be ashamed of yourself! Surely you're not frightened of an old woman and two teenagers?'

Mackay stood stony-faced, doing his best to ignore her. Oblivious to the gun, Christie's grandmother took a step forward and poked him in the chest with her forefinger:

'You won't get away with this, you know. My neighbours will miss us first thing tomorrow and then there'll be a hue and cry, I can tell you!'

'They won't miss you if your car's gone and they think you and the lass have taken off for the day,' said Mackay coldly. 'Now, I would strongly recommend you to sit down and shut up — then I won't have to hurt you . . . or the kids.' He put out a hand to nudge her away but Christie's grandmother brushed it aside.

'Don't you *dare* touch me!' she spat, returning to her place on the ground. She was shaking with rage.

Bill Davidson attempted once more to sit up. This time he succeeded. He looked around the cave, his eyes still only half-focused. Slowly and painfully comprehension began to register on his face.

'Mackay, you bastard! What the hell did you do that for?' He rubbed the back of his head.

Mackay edged back until he was standing directly in the entrance, commanding a full view of the interior of the cave. He swung his torch in an arc, pausing briefly as the beam came to rest, one by one, on the faces of his four captives.

'To keep you quiet while we wait for a boat,' he replied. 'It'll be along in due course, so just settle down there. I want no trouble and I'll give you no trouble.' He stepped forward and drew an imaginary line across the floor with his heel, then returned to the cave-mouth. 'But I'll shoot anyone who comes closer than that. Understood?'

'Where are you taking us?' Bill Davidson persisted.

'You'll find out. Now don't waste your breath.' He extinguished the torch and squatted down in the cave-mouth, a black silhouette against the lesser blackness of the night outside.

'Mr Davidson?' It was Christie's grandmother.

There was a grunted acknowledgement in the darkness.

'Perhaps you'd be so good as to tell me what's going on?'

'There's not a lot to tell really. Except that they seem to have got us stitched up in here.' The indignation with which he had addressed Mackay had gone. Now his voice sounded tired, deflated.

'But why, Mr Davidson? Would you please tell me that.'

'Because, as your grand-daughter and my son will tell you, I've been conned. For the first time in my life, conned rotten. Mackay, Ross and Ross's son are part of the People's Army of Alba. They're terrorists, Mrs McKenzie.'

'And what's that got to do with Christie and me?' Her voice contained a note of impatience.

There was a pause, then he continued: 'Christie and Tom discovered them. They're planning to blow up the NATO fuel depot at Aultbea. They found out that we knew and now they're taking steps to . . . put us out of the way . . . while they do it, I suppose. They couldn't take your grand-daughter without you noticing that she'd gone. So they took you too.'

'Is this true, Christie?'

'I'm afraid so, Nan,' Christie replied, feeling all of a sudden terribly guilty. 'I'm sorry.'

'Nonsense, child! I'm sure you did just the right thing.

But, Mr Davidson, I don't quite understand you. If you knew, why in the name of God did you not contact the police?'

'We didn't have time,' he replied. 'Tom and Christie only found out this evening. They came to tell me. I wasn't convinced. I wanted to make my own enquiries first. But somehow they realised we might be onto them. I think maybe they were hanging around the cabin, and . . . well . . . you know the rest.'

That was not the whole truth, thought Christie, feeling angry and betrayed. She was about to interject but Tom beat her to it:

'There *was* time, Dad. But you said NOT to tell the . . .'

'Christ, boy, you can be stupid sometimes! Of course, I did. I'm running a political party. I'm not going to go round turning my own members in to the police until I'm absolutely sure that they're in the wrong. Think of the publicity!'

'Well,' said Christie's grandmother, 'it's too late now. It doesn't seem there's a lot we can do.'

'Not a great deal,' said Bill Davidson morosely. He lapsed into silence.

'So tell me how you did find out,' said Christie's grandmother softly. Between them, Tom and Christie related what had happened.

'It was a pity you didn't tell me,' she said, without recrimination. 'I'd never met the Mackay laddie before tonight, but I'd heard enough about him. No one round here trusts him. I'd've been onto Sergeant Drummond at Ullapool in a flash.' She paused, then lowering her voice, said: 'And how on earth did he manage to get mixed up with these two in the first place?'

'They're running the local branch of Alba Nova for him,' said Christie.

'I gathered that, but why them?'

'I guess because he was too wrapped up in his ideas to notice who he was dealing with,' said Tom. 'And he thought they'd just do exactly what he told them to. Everyone else does.'

Christie's grandmother made no comment.

An hour or so later Christie was awoken by Tom shaking her shoulder.

'The boat's coming,' he whispered.

She rolled over, suddenly aware of the bitter cold which seemed to have penetrated her bones. She was stiff, too, from the floor of the cave which was covered with a deep layer of sheep droppings, impacted over the years into a solid surface a little more yielding than bare earth, but considerably harder than sand.

She sat up and peered closely at the faint luminosity of her watch dial. One-thirty am. Her grandmother had her back propped against the cave wall, her head lolling to one side. From time to time she shivered in her sleep. Bill Davidson sat apart, his arms clasped around his knees which were drawn up under his chin, lost in thought.

Out in the darkness over Mackay's shoulder there was a faint glow rolling crazily from side to side. It was too dim to be a navigation light, but it could be from the wheelhouse of a small fishing boat. The glow grew a little larger and then halted. A couple of minutes later a dark figure appeared beside Mackay in the cave mouth.

'OK everyone,' said Mackay getting to his feet. 'Time to go.'

Christie shook her grandmother gently and she lifted her head with a start. Tom and his father were already standing.

'Two at a time,' said Mackay, pointing the gun at Christie and her grandmother. 'You two,' he shifted to the Davidsons, 'sit down again.'

Christie and her grandmother stepped out of the cave and followed Ross's son down the beach to where a black rubber dinghy rocked on a line of foam at the water's edge. They climbed in and grasped the rope handles set into its sides as he gunned the outboard and took the dinghy bucking through the short, powerful breakers between the beach and the mouth of the cove where a small, snub-nosed lobster-boat wallowed at anchor.

At their approach the wheelhouse door opened and Ross emerged, looking more lugubrious than ever with his long face peering out from beneath the dripping brim of a black sou'wester. His son brought the dinghy alongside and Ross reached down to haul first her grandmother, then Christie, unceremoniously aboard. They were both soaked to the skin.

Tom and his father arrived a few minutes later and were herded into the wheelhouse to join Christie, her grandmother and Ross. The little timber cabin was designed for two people in comfort, three at a pinch. With five occupants it was almost unbearable, full of stale pipe smoke and the smell of diesel. Christie jammed herself up against the sliding door and tugged Tom towards her, trying to make as much space as she could for her grandmother who was looking distinctly pale.

Mackay slid back the opposite door and poked his head in.

'Bit of a squeeze in there, is it? Well you can thank your stars you're not travelling deck class like Kevin and me. And don't get any ideas about taking over from Bertie. We'll be watching you. OK, Bertie, take her away.' He closed the door and disappeared into the darkness on deck.

The albatross grasped the wheel and eased open the throttle. The engine, which had been idling, began to throb as the lobster-boat swung round and nosed out into Gruinard Bay. As she cleared the mouth of the cove the full force of the gale caught her, buffeting and rattling the wheelhouse as her bows lifted on the peaks and thudded down into the troughs of the short, steep waves which followed one another in such close succession that it began to seem as if the boat must be remaining stationary, trapped on some ghastly fairground device.

Through the sleet-blurred windscreen, Christie could just

see the occasional streak of grey-white froth lining the crest of another approaching wave. All around, though, was pitch darkness. Where could they be going, she wondered, clutching at the door handle as the bows slammed down and the engine screamed for a moment, the propellor spinning free of the water. She glanced at her grandmother and prayed it wasn't the Summer Isles, six or seven miles out on the edge of The Minch — one of the most unpredictable stretches of water in the world.

Her grandmother was standing next to the albatross, her hands braced on the edge of a small chart table beside the wheel. Her face was white and drawn and her eyelids fluttered with the effort of remaining on her feet. She wouldn't be able to stand a journey that long, thought Christie. She doubted whether the boat would either, come to that. Every timber and plate seemed to be creaking and groaning in a chorus of protest.

Tom was the first to succumb. Christie saw him swallowing down the bile as his face turned greyish-green. Then he lurched for the door. Christie yanked it open, wincing at the blast of freezing air which invaded the wheelhouse, and hung onto the back of his coat as he leant out into the wind, his shoulders heaving. After a few moments he straightened up, wiping his face on his sleeve and took a pace backwards into the cabin.

A minute or two later Christie also was sick. Shivering as she retched downwind, she caught a glimpse of a dark figure squatting on the deck, aft of the wheelhouse, but she felt too ill to wonder which of them it was. At length she pulled her head back into the cabin to hear Bill Davidson exclaim: 'This is insanity! Where the hell are you taking us, man?'

He sounded more desperate than angry and Christie was surprised to notice that he seemed to have shrunk, as if all his bullish energy had deserted him.

Bertie Ross gripped the wheel with both hands, an empty pipe clenched between his teeth, and stared straight ahead.

'Not far. It'll not be long now,' he replied. He began to

turn the wheel to starboard and little by little the boat edged round until she was taking the sea almost full on her beam. Now the waves were breaking over the deck and smashing into the wheelhouse at Christie's side as the boat shuddered and rolled on her new course.

Bill Davidson suddenly heaved open the opposite door and leaned out. At the same moment the boat heeled sharply to starboard and he lurched forward. Ross's right arm shot out and grabbed the tail of his oilskin just in time to stop him vanishing into the darkness.

'Bloody fool!' Ross muttered as Tom's father hauled himself back into the cabin, green-faced, and slid the door closed. 'There's a bucket under the bench. Use that.' Bill Davidson fumbled for the bucket and bent over it, his back turned to the others.

Christie stared ahead, trying to ignore the oily coating of nausea in her stomach and at the same time to blot out the image of the great black wave, twice as big as the rest, which was lurking in wait for them like a water-kelpie, somewhere out there in the darkness.

They'd been at sea for twenty minutes, she calculated, maybe half an hour, sailing straight out into Gruinard Bay. Now they'd turned at right angles to their original course. There was only one place they could possibly be heading for — Gruinard Island. She felt a momentary chill which had nothing to with the big black wave.

It was what they had done to the sheep that Christie had always found most macabre — herded them *en masse* over a cliff and then bulldozed the cliff down on top of them, burying their contaminated carcases under hundreds of tons of earth and sandstone rubble. That was back in 1943 when the War Department had chosen Gruinard Island for biological warfare experiments: the place had been deliberately infected with anthrax and the island's sheep had become so maddened by the disease that their gruesome mass execution had become the only possible way to dispose of them.

For forty-five years afterwards Gruinard Island had remained a no-go area, its beaches strung with barbed wire and skull-and-crossbones sign; lurid warnings were posted at all possible embarkation points on the mainland. Then, last year, the Ministry of Defence had pronounced it safe and offered it back to its original owners. The warning signs and barbed wire had been removed. But Christie had not yet heard of a single local setting foot on the place. 'You wouldn't catch me there,' Willie McLeod the postman had said to her grandmother, just the other day. 'It has a dead look to it.'

There was a rapping at the door beside her. Christie opened it a few inches and Mackay put his head in, accompanied by an icy draught.

'How're we doing?' he asked.

'Five minutes,' grunted the albatross.

'Thank God!' muttered Bill Davidson as Mackay's head retreated. His face was the colour of chalk. So was Tom's and, Christie suspected, her own. Her grandmother, the only one who had not been sick, looked equally unwell but there was a waxiness to her pallor which Christie found disturbing. Little drops of sweat glistened on her upper lip and a vein pumped visibly through the translucent skin at her temple. Her eyes were closed and her knuckles bluish-white where she grasped the edge of the chart table.

Now the boat was beginning to lose speed. Ross had loosened his rigid grasp of the wheel and was gentling it through some obviously tricky manoeuvre, a degree to port, a couple of degrees to starboard, back to port, a little more . . . the wind was easing and the waves dropping . . . Ross slid back the throttle . . . the appalling corkscrewing motion died away . . . there was a rattle of chains and the boat slewed to a halt.

Mackay was at the door again.

'Women and children first!' He gesticulated at Christie and her grandmother who opened her eyes and looked at the door, a dazed expression on her face.

'C'mon, Nan!' Christie held out her hand. Her grandmother took it and stepped unsteadily out of the wheelhouse, gasping as the cold hit her. Mackay grasped her by the arm and led her, none too gently, along the swaying, slippery deck.

Kevin was waiting in the dinghy which bobbed like a black slug alongside the stern. A cloud of exhaust poured from the outboard as he tried to keep level with the wallowing lobster-boat. Christie waited till the dinghy rose, then scrambled in and turned round to extend a hand to her grandmother. Mackay grasped her round the waist, waited till the dinghy rose again then heaved her off her feet and swung her down. Christie grabbed one frail arm and tried to support her as her feet met the duckboards in the bottom of the boat, but her grandmother was too heavy and they both collapsed in a heap on the floor. Christie heard a soft grunt of pain.

By the time they had disentangled themselves the dinghy was lurching in the shallows. A wave broke over the stern, sousing them all as Kevin hopped out and held the little craft steady with the painter. Christie and her grandmother stumbled for'ard and stepped onto dry land.

They walked a few paces up the pebbled beach and sat down, shivering. Christie's grandmother rubbed her shin, then grasped Christie's arm and sqeezed it. 'Oh, Christie, Christie,' she said weakly. 'I'm too old for all this.'

A minute later the dinghy returned with Tom and his father. This time Mackay was at the outboard. They disembarked and walked up the beach.

'Welcome to Gruinard Island!' said Mackay as they halted.

Bill Davidson's eyes widened in horror.

'Good God Almighty, Mackay! You're going to leave us here? The place is poisoned!'

'Not any longer,' he replied. 'At least that's what the Ministry of Defence say. Ask them if you want!' He was grinning. 'Well, enjoy your stay. You'll be taken off sometime tomorrow night.' He turned to go. 'Oh, and here, I nearly forgot — some provisions. We don't want you starving.' He unslung a canvas bag from his shoulder and dropped it on the pebbles.

'Mr Mackay!' called Christie's grandmother. Her voice sounded tremulous and old.

'Yes?'

'Might I ask what is to prevent us from going straight to the police once we have been . . . taken off, as you put it?'

'Oh dear!' said Mackay with mock concern. 'Has no one told you? I think you'd better have a chat with Mr Davidson. He's a very wealthy man, you know . . .'

He strode back to the dinghy and piloted it out to the lobster-boat. The glow from the wheelhouse began to dwindle and five minutes later there was nothing but the roaring, sleet-filled darkness.

Chapter 9

'We can't stay here all night. We'll freeze to death!' It was
Tom who spoke first.

Christie came alert, realising that the intense cold had
reduced her almost to a state of trance. Her jeans were
sodden and the water seemed even to have penetrated her
tightly-buttoned oilskin. Her teeth were chattering and
already her fingers were unpleasantly devoid of sensation.
Beside her, her grandmother was rocking back and forth in
silent endurance with her arms wrapped tightly across her
chest.

Christie scrambled to her feet and turned to scan the
beach. She could dimly discern a shallow sweep of pebbles,
apparently devoid of shelter apart from the short pro-
montory at its northern end, in whose lee the lobster-boat
had anchored. Immediately behind the beach the ground
sloped upwards and vanished into the darkness.

She tried to visualise the island. She'd seen it often enough
— every day in fact: a long, brown slab lying level with the
opposite tip of the bay, three miles across from Mellon
Udrigle and a mile from the far shore. They must be on its
west-facing shore, she reckoned — that was where their
dog-leg course from the prayer-cave would have landed

them. If they made for the southern end they would surely find somewhere more sheltered. And they'd be nearer the mainland. Maybe they could signal for help.

'I think we should go down to the end,' she said, pointing southwards. 'Try and find some shelter.'

'No! We stay here!' A trace of the former bullishness had returned to Bill Davidson's voice, but it failed to mask his anxiety. 'The place is a death-trap!'

Christie's grandmother lifted her head and with the greatest effort, said: 'Mr Davidson, Dougal Mackay may be the most reprehensible scoundrel you have ever met but he was at least telling the truth about Gruinard Island. It was declared safe last year. Believe that or not, as you choose, but I am going down to the end with Christie if I can. There are caves there — I used to come here when I was a girl, before they contaminated the place — and I very badly need to get out of this wind. If I do not, Mr Davidson, you may find yourself with a case of hypothermia on your hands, along with your other troubles.' She struggled to her feet and held out her hand for Christie, then set off down the beach without a backward glance.

Raised voices carried faintly downwind towards them and a few moments later Tom panted out of the darkness, his feet scrunching on the pebbles. He placed himself on the far side of Christie's grandmother and took her arm.

'He's coming,' he yelled across the wind.

'What did you say to him?' shouted Christie.

'That it was time he realised he doesn't have all the answers.'

For half an hour they stumbled through the darkness, their hands and faces numb from the biting wind and sleet. Where possible they kept to the pebbly beaches of the coves which indented the shoreline; but in places their progress was barred by a headland or a treacherous jumble of black, seaweed-covered rocks. Then they turned inland and climbed, thankful for the torch which Christie had remembered was still in her oilskin pocket.

Her grandmother's breathing was becoming increasingly painful and shallow; in the torchlight her face was grey and beaded with sweat. Christie and Tom found themselves taking a little more of her weight with each step.

Tom's father plodded behind them, his eyes on the ground. He did not offer to help.

'Are you all right, Nan?' Christie asked, putting her face close to her grandmother's ear.

'Yes, dear, I can manage if you can.' Her voice was almost inaudible and she screwed up her face with the effort of speaking. 'I think it's the next bay, maybe the one after.'

They descended a heathery slope, slipping and sliding on the damp roots, and stepped onto the pebbles of another cove. Christie walked a few paces ahead, playing the torch along the rear of the beach. Towards the far end the ground rose into a bank, too low to merit the description of cliff. Clumps of heather waved frenetically along its lip and at its foot was a small dark opening.

'There's one!' she shouted, running on and stooping as she passed through its entrance.

In the torchlight this cave seemed somewhat smaller than the prayer-cave, but its proportions were better. It was roughly circular with a domed roof which rose to a point some ten or twelve feet above the solid rock floor, in whose centre lay the blackened ashes and charred wood of an old fire — a very old fire, it seemed likely.

There was something else that distinguished this cave from the prayer-cave and for a moment Christie could not think what it was. Then she realised. It was bone dry and the air was almost still. She looked back at the entrance and saw what she had not noticed as she came in: there was a very short passage, a sort of curved vestibule like the sawn-off spout of a teapot, between the chamber of the cave and the beach. From where she stood she could see only a thin sliver of the darkness outside. The cave itself was almost completely insulated from the elements.

Christie's grandmother stepped into the torchlight. She gave a little 'Ouf!' of exhaustion and sank to the ground, her eyes closed. Tom came in close behind her and a moment later Bill Davidson arrived. He glanced cursorily at his surroundings, then sat down with a grunt and put his head in his hands.

'We need a fire,' said Tom, looking with concern at Christie's grandmother whose whole body was now shaking uncontrollably with cold. 'Quickly,' he added. 'Has anyone got any matches?'

Christie was certain she didn't but felt in her pockets, just in case. Nothing there. She bent down and searched the pockets of her grandmother's coat. No.

Bill Davidson didn't seem to have heard his son's request. 'Have you got any matches, Dad?' Tom reiterated. His father looked up briefly, fished in his pocket and threw over a box of Swan Vestas.

'OK, let's go and see if we can find something to burn,' said Tom. He and Christie went outside into the gale.

During the forty-five years in which it had been uninhabited, Gruinard Island had accumulated a vast store of the sea's somewhat haphazard bounty. Bits of rubber tyre, oilcans, shoes, plastic bottles, virtually anything that floated, including copious driftwood, littered the high-water mark. It took them no more than a few minutes to gather an armful each of bleached planking, sections of smashed wooden pallet and shards of packing case.

On the way back to the cave Christie shouted:

'Something's happened to your dad, hasn't it?'

Tom nodded.

'What?'

'I dunno,' he yelled back. 'Some kind of shock, I think.'

'D'you know what's going on?'

'No, but they had a long conversation with him before they took us away from the cabin. I wasn't allowed to hear.'

'I think we'd better try and find out.'

'Yes, I think we had.'

Returning to the cave they dumped the wood on the floor and searched for something combustible to start the fire. Christie produced a couple of crumpled Kleenex and Tom, somewhat sheepishly, an empty cigarette packet which he placed amongst the old ashes. Bill Davidson, when prompted, pulled a small notebook from inside his coat and tore out a few pages.

The paper, together with some slivers of the driest driftwood which Tom had carefully sliced off with a penknife, caught swiftly. Within five minutes the walls and roof of the cave were dancing with firelight. There was a good deal of smoke but it seemed a small discomfort to bear for the luxurious warmth which was starting slowly to seep through their damp, frozen bodies.

Tom opened the bag Mackay had left them. It contained a thermos of tea, a sliced white loaf, an open packet of processed cheese, half-a-dozen rather bruised apples and a large bar of chocolate from which several squares had already gone. It looked, thought Christie, as if someone had hurriedly raided their own larder for this. It was certainly not what she would have put together for four people for a twenty-four hour stay on an uninhabited island. Why had they bothered at all? Why hadn't they just killed them? And what *had* happened to Tom's father . . . ?

'Tea?' Tom was proffering the thermos mug.

Christie took it gratefully and sipped, then turned to her grandmother whose shivering had eased a little. She held the mug to the pale, almost bluish lips. Without opening her eyes her grandmother lifted her hands and clasped them round the mug as she drank.

'Thank you, dear,' she said feebly. 'I think I'll sleep a little now.' Her hands fell back in her lap.

'Yes, Nan,' said Christie, trying to keep the alarm from her voice. 'Are you warm enough?'

'Maybe I'll get a bit closer.' She struggled to stand up but her legs seemed unwilling to bear her weight. Tom and

Christie helped move her along the wall until she was as close to the fire as safety allowed. Tom took off his coat and laid it over her. Her head lolled forward, trailing wisps of white hair.

For a moment the two of them stood looking at her in anxious silence. Then Tom whispered:

'We've done all we can.'

'Yes, I suppose so,' Christie agreed reluctantly. She turned away and glanced at the provisions.

'Do you want something to eat?' she asked.

Tom put his hand to his stomach and pulled a face.

'Me neither,' said Christie. The idea of food seemed to bring the nausea back. 'Mr Davidson?'

Tom's father shook his head.

'What now?' Christie asked.

'Get some sleep, if I were you,' Tom's father grunted.

Tom and Christie looked at one another. Tom shrugged and nodded. There didn't seem much else they could do and Christie felt herself in no mood for a conversation with Tom's father now.

She lay down facing the fire. Her damp jeans clung to her legs and the rock was hard at her hip and shoulder, but she felt suddenly so tired that she scarcely noticed the discomfort.

'Goodnight,' Tom whispered from the other side of the fire.

'Goodnight,' she replied drowsily.

Tom's father was snoring heavily. Christie lay with her eyes closed and her mind fuzzy with sleep. It was a most irritating noise; but she didn't quite dare to reach across and give him the requisite prod.

After a while she opened her eyes. The fire had almost died away, leaving a bed of white ash in which glowed a handful of embers. The air in the cave had grown chilly again. Christie placed some more wood on the embers and blew them to life. She glanced at her grandmother and was relieved to see that she had fallen into a deeper, more peaceful sleep in which her chest rose and fell, gently and rhythmically. She drew up the coat which had slipped down her grandmother's body, then sat back and gazed into the flames.

It was like watching some mesmerising ballet in which the dancers shrank and grew, leaping and tripping and side-stepping, their robes white at one moment, orange the next, then dull red, crimson, blue . . . The more fiercely the fire burned the more fevered and elaborate became the dance.

Christie began to feel light-headed. She turned away for a moment then glanced back at the very centre of the fire where there was little movement, just a blaze of white heat. Quite suddenly she felt a sharp tug inside, as if she had missed her footing in some dangerous place, then she was no longer looking into the fire, but staring straight through it to a dim landscape of heather and boulders which swirled with snow in the failing light.

There was no sign of life here and yet Christie was filled with a strange sense of expectancy. Something would happen if she watched long enough, she was certain of it. The snow continued to flurry, settling like a dusting of icing sugar on the heather and whitening the hump-backed boulders.

From the left there came a man, running. His head was down and the hood of his coat was pulled up so she couldn't see his face but she could sense the fear that drove him through the bleak grey dusk. He was being pursued.

For fully a minute Christie looked on as the man forged through the deep, snow-sprinkled heather, dodging around boulders and leaping burns. He was growing tired. She could almost hear him panting now but still she could not see his face. His coat flapped open as he ran. Christie caught a dim glimpse of tartan lining and a bulging poacher's pocket. His foot struck an obstacle. He staggered, collected himself and ran on, ignoring the large yellow flashlight that had tumbled from the pocket.

Now the land was beginning to rise. He was stumbling up the slope of an escarpment. Ahead of him stood a large and grotesquely-shaped boulder which resembled the face of an old crone with deep set eyes, a hooked nose and jutting chin. He ran towards it and as he drew closer Christie could see that, just beyond, the land fell away sharply in a steep bank or cliff. Now he was almost level with the boulder. A couple more paces and he was approaching the lip of the escarpment, glancing to left and right. There was a faint cry from somewhere to his right. He stopped and spun round, his features blurred by the falling snow. Immediately a shot rang out. He lurched back a pace, throwing out his arms, and fell from view.

For a moment Christie's gaze remained fixed on the face of the old crone. Then it was gone and she was looking into the white heart of the fire.

The trembling crept up on her slowly, no more than a flutter in her belly to start with but gradually gathering strength until the dragon's breath was shuddering through her in hot and cold squalls which made her hands rattle in her lap. With it came the panic.

I'm all right. It's just another part of me that I've got to get used to, she told herself, trying to remember the conversation with her grandmother. But it didn't seem to work. Her heartbeat had doubled. The cave suddenly felt small and suffocating. She had to get outside. She climbed to her feet and was tiptoe-ing over her grandmother's sleeping body when a whisper came from the other side of the fire:

'Christie! Are you all right?'

'Yes . . . no . . . I've got to get some air!' She squeezed past the fire, stepped over Tom's legs and dashed outside, gulping in the chill, salt air as she strode down the beach. The wind had dropped right away and now it was snowing heavily, the large pale flakes drifting silently, endlessly through the dim grey of approaching dawn.

She heard footsteps behind her, then Tom's hand was on her arm.

'Christie!' There was concern in his voice.

She turned to him and nodded but said nothing. They walked for some time in silence and eventually Christie began to feel the panic receding. There was something reassuring about Tom's presence, the physical contact of his hand at her elbow.

At length they returned to the cave, their hair and shoulders glistening with melting snowflakes. Christie's grandmother shifted in her sleep as they entered. Bill Davidson lay full length against the far wall, snoring rhythmically. Tom put more wood on the fire and they sat down, flames flickering on the shadowy walls.

'You saw something, didn't you?' he said softly.

Christie looked at him. 'I didn't think you believed in all that.'

'I do now. I watched it happening to you. Your whole face changed while you were looking into the fire, as if you were ... sitting here, but *living* somewhere else. And the look on you when you got up — it was just like at the beach that day.' He paused, then added: 'It scares you, doesn't it?'

She nodded. 'But I suppose I've got to get used to it — it seems it's part of me.'

'What did you see ... I mean ... is it OK to tell me?'

'I think I saw someone being murdered,' she said slowly.

'Jesus!' said Tom. 'Really?'

'Yes. There was this man running through a snowstorm, somewhere up in the hills, I think. Then there was a shot and he ... just fell ... fell over a cliff.'

'Do you know who it was?'

'No, I never really saw his face.'

'What will you do?'

'What can I do?' She shrugged. 'It may have happened already, for all I know. Anyway, we're here aren't we ...' she spread out her arms to encompass the cave, '. . . marooned.'

They fell silent. After a while Tom moved closer to Christie and put his arm around her. It was an awkward, unpractised gesture; but Christie felt a sudden tiny flow of warmth and an easing of the knot in her stomach.

'I'd be scared too, you know,' he said.

She thought a little, then said: 'If I could use it . . . I mean . . . to help the people I see, I suppose it would be better.'

'But you did,' said Tom. 'You made sure the boat got out quickly the other day.'

'Yes, maybe. But this is different. I don't know who he is, where he is, or even whether he's alive. In any case, my getting the boat out didn't prevent them capsizing. You see, I don't think it allows me to . . . change anything. I just see it happening, that's all. And I don't want to see these things, Tom.' She could feel the tears coming and she buried her face on his shoulder.

Tom tightened his arm around her. 'Maybe that's all you're meant to do,' he said at length.

'Maybe,' she sniffed. She broke away from him and forced a wan smile. 'Pretty rotten timing, though!'

'I'll say!' He grinned sympathetically. 'So what *are* we going to do?'

'I don't know. What do you reckon?'

Tom gazed into the fire for a while, then looked across to his father.

'I think we should try and get a bit more sleep, then have a word with *him*. There's a lot of this that doesn't make much sense to me.'

'Me neither,' Christie agreed.

'One thing's for sure, though.'

'What's that?'

'I don't fancy being stuck here until tomorrow night.'

'Nor do I,' said Christie, her mind filling suddenly with an image of woolly bodies dropping from the edge of a cliff like large, untidy snowflakes.

When she awoke again the cave was still in semi-darkness. She glanced at her watch and was startled to see that it was nearly eleven in the morning and the others were still asleep.

The curving mouth of the cave admitted no more than a thin splinter of daylight, she realised; not nearly enough to disturb its four exhausted occupants.

She got stiffly to her feet and shook Tom awake. Together they went outside and walked along the beach to get warm.

The snow continued to fall and the waters of the bay lay dull and still. Directly opposite them was the curve of the mainland shore. The cloud hung low, but the snow lay lower still, splitting the landscape neatly in two along a horizontal line, a hundred feet or so above sea-level.

Over to their right was Laide and further round still, Mellon Udrigle. There was a dusting of white along the hummocks of the peninsula.

'I've never seen snow at Mellon Udrigle!' Christie said. 'I don't think I've ever seen it that low on the mainland, either — not even in winter, let alone the end of April.'

'It must be the greenhouse effect,' said Tom.

'I thought that made things hotter.'

'Maybe it's the ozone layer, then. It's bound to be one or the other. My dad knows all about it, from his farming, I suppose. And it's one of the main . . . whaddo-they-call-it . . . platforms for Alba Nova. Anyway, he says we're in a real mess.'

'He's right about that,' said Christie, glancing towards the cave. 'And I think it's him that's in the biggest mess.'

Tom nodded thoughtfully as they turned round and made their way back.

Christie's grandmother was awake when they returned. She still looked pale but her eyes no longer seemed glazed and the bluish tinge had left her lips.

'How do you feel, Nan?' asked Christie anxiously.

'I'd have slept better in my bed.' She smiled ruefully and rubbed her shoulders. 'I'm all right, though. A wee bit stiff. But I'll live!'

Christie bent down and kissed her warmly. 'Thank goodness!' she exclaimed. 'You gave us a fright last night, you know, Nan!'

'What, me? Never!'

'Yes, you, Nan! Anyway, you're really OK now? Cross your heart?'

'Cross my heart!'

'Would you like some breakfast, Mrs McKenzie,' asked Tom.

'That would be grand. What do we have — porridge, poached eggs, toast?'

'Bread and cheese, I'm afraid.'

'Ah, survival rations, is it? Well, I suppose sccastaways can't be choosers!'

Tom built up the fire again while Christie laid out the provisions.

'We'd better go easy in case we *are* here till tonight,' she said.

Her grandmother sniffed. 'We'll find a way to get off, don't you worry!'

At that moment Bill Davidson awoke. He sat up with a start and looked around him, his face creasing in a deep frown as his whereabouts dawned on him.

'God, that was uncomfortable,' he said, rubbing his legs and arms. His eye fell on the provisions and he grimaced. 'Is that breakfast?'

Christie nodded.

'And lunch, and tea, I suppose?'

'We won't be needing lunch or tea,' said Christie's grandmother sharply.

'Oh? And why not?'

'Because we're going to get off this island, Mr Davidson. We're going to get ourselves to the mainland and then I'm going straight to the police.'

He leant forward and glared at Christie's grandmother across the fire. The sleep appeared to have restored some of his energy and the cold, hard look had returned to his eyes.

'You,' he said, jabbing his forefinger at her, 'are not going anywhere. Nor the kids. And nor am I.'

'Why not?'

'Because I say so.'

'Mr Davidson,' Christie's grandmother's voice was icy, 'you are obviously a man accustomed to giving orders. But let me suggest to you now the boot is somewhat on the other foot. First, you have got us into this situation and you have more than a passing duty to get us out of it. Second,' she was ticking off the points on her fingers, 'I am not accustomed to taking orders and I fully intend to get back to the mainland. Third, I know this place. You do not and you would be well advised to listen to me.'

'No!' He slammed his fist into his palm. 'You listen to me! Those men are dangerous and they'll kill if they have to. We're bloody lucky to be still alive and we'd be mad to try and escape. Don't you think they'll be keeping an eye out?'

'So why *didn't* they kill us?' She returned his stare.

'Because . . .'

'Because,' Tom interrupted, 'you made some kind of a deal with them . . .'

'How dare you!' He turned to Tom, his eyes blazing. 'You keep out of this, or else . . .'

'No, I won't keep out of it,' said Tom defiantly. 'It concerns me just as much as you, not to mention the people in Aultbea who are going to get burning diesel and bits of fuel tank on their heads. Very ecological!'

His father bridled but Tom ignored him and continued: 'I think you agreed not to interfere, not to try and escape or tell the police, so long as they didn't harm us. What else could you have been talking about before they took us down to the cave?'

Bill Davidson's face turned white with anger. He clenched his fists and for a moment Christie thought he was going to hit his son.

'You've got a damned cheek . . .' he began, but Christie's grandmother broke in:

'Did you do that, Mr Davidson?' she said quietly. 'Did you make a deal with them?'

'Of course I didn't,' he said curtly.

'So why did Dougal Mackay suggest we had a chat with you? And what did he mean by saying that you were a wealthy man? That you would buy our silence, maybe? Why, Mr Davidson? Why are you prepared to sit back and let them wreak their havoc, maybe kill people? I don't believe for a moment that you're in sympathy with them.'

'No, I'm not. And the rest is no concern of yours!' He was blustering now. Christie could see a vein pulsing nervously at his throat.

'Ah, but it is,' continued her grandmother, 'because if you did strike a bargain with them you're effectively keeping the rest of us here against our will. And that's a crime. It makes you their accomplice.'

For some time he stared silently at the fire, then sat back with a deep sigh:

'So I came to an agreement. Is that what you wanted to hear?'

'Yes,' said Tom. 'But why?'

His father shook his head wearily. 'You wouldn't understand.'

Tom flushed and glared angrily across the fire. 'Stop treating me like some kind of halfwit! I'm fed up with you criticising me just because I'm not what you want me to be. Well, it's you that's fouled up this time. You owe me . . . you owe us . . . a decent explanation.'

His father's face registered a fleeting look of astonishment. He recovered himself quickly and tried to smile but it fell away at the corners of his mouth as he said:

'OK, son. You're right, I should explain: Mackay and Ross conned me — as you know . . .'

'I should say they did,' interrupted Christie's grandmother. 'Quarrying and fish-farming, neither of them the most conservational of professions.'

Bill Davidson glared at her. 'That was intentional. A publicity ploy. We were planning to make a documentary about Green converts. Mackay and Ross were to be two of the subjects. We were going to finance them to change their activities.'

Christie's grandmother snorted. 'So that's how it's done, these days.'

He ignored her and continued: 'As I was saying, they were using Alba Nova as a cover for their PAA activities. That was bad enough, but what was worse was that they've been fiddling the local Alba Nova books and using our funds — my own personal money, in fact — to buy their explosives and other equipment.'

'So why couldn't you just turn them in?' asked Christie.

'Because,' he continued impatiently, 'if it ever got out, that would be the end of Alba Nova — and my political career. The publicity would kill us stone dead. No one would take a party seriously that had allowed a bunch of terrorists to slip in the back door and start misappropriating its funds. You can see that, can't you?'

Tom nodded. 'So I was right. You don't try and stop them blowing up the fuel dump. You promise not to let on afterwards and Alba Nova keeps going. They agree not to kill us. But they stick us here, out of harm's way, just for good measure . . .'

'With the cars hidden away in Bertie's quarry so everyone thinks we're away for a day or two . . .' Christie added.

Tom's father nodded.

'So why did they hit you when we got to the cave?' asked Tom.

He shrugged. 'I'm not quite sure. Partly to show that they meant business. Partly so that I wouldn't cause any trouble while the two Rosses were off collecting Christie and Mrs McKenzie.'

'But I'm still not quite clear why they didn't just kill us,' said Christie's grandmother. 'It would have saved them a lot of trouble.'

Bill Davidson gave a wry grin. 'They couldn't. You see they've already been publicly identified with me — through Alba Nova. They would have been the prime suspects. And

I imagine they want to carry on doing what they're doing.'

'Well I suppose we should count ourselves lucky for that,' she agreed. 'Thank you for being frank with us, Mr Davidson. But we're not going to let them carry on doing what they're doing, are we!'

'Oh God! You still don't understand, do you.' He pounded the rock in frustration. 'We've *got* to sit it out! Alba Nova could be the first really good thing that's happened to Scotland since the Act of Union. Look! It's not just my political career, it's the future of *our* country we're talking about. There's a general election next year. People here are fed up with things being run from London, especially by that *woman*. They're ripe for self-government. The Scot Nats are all over the place and we're in with a real chance. We can't throw it all away now. We can't!'

'And for that you'd offer me money,' asked Christie's grandmother in quiet amazement, 'to sit back and keep mum while a handful of . . . madmen blow up a hillside, endangering the lives of several hundred people. For a political ideal?'

'Yes, I would!'

'Then it seems to me,' she said coldly, 'that you are a very confused man, Mr Davidson. Until you can re-arrange your priorities in some more humane fashion, I have nothing more to say to you.' She rose awkwardly to her feet. 'Now, I'm going outside to have a look around — to see what I can remember about this place.'

'I'll come with you,' said Christie, glad of a respite from the charged atmosphere within the cave. She got up and glanced at Tom but he shook his head and returned his attention to his father who was staring into the embers, his large hands flexing restlessly on his knees.

The expression on Tom's face, she realised as she followed her grandmother out of the cave, was almost one of sympathy.

Chapter 10

'Is it really *that* important to you, Dad?'

Tom unscrewed the cap of the thermos and handed across a mug of lukewarm tea. His father took it without lifting his gaze from the fire. When at length he replied, his voice was distant: 'Yes, it is.'

'But I don't understand . . . people are going to get killed . . .'

There was no reply.

'Tell me! You've got to! I'm your son for Chrissake. And we're in this together.' Tom's voice was rising.

His father looked up wearily and said:

'I came out of National Service with two ambitions in life, son — to make a lot of money and to go into politics. I've achieved the first. Now I'm going for the the second.'

Tom paused, waiting for further explanation. But none came. 'Is that it, then? So you can be a hotshot . . . on the TV . . . in the papers?'

'No, Goddamnit! I have beliefs.'

'Well, what are they?'

His father straightened his shoulders. 'Is this some kind of inquisition?'

'Jesus, Dad! I-just-want-to-understand!'

'OK, OK.' He held up his hands. 'Listen, for years Scotland's been run by a bunch of city-slickers in London who've never been north of Watford, who don't understand our country, don't even like it, but are still prepared to take everything they can get from it. I want to see the place run by the Scots, for the Scots.'

'And what about the ecology bit?'

'That's something far bigger than party, or even national politics. It's simply the most important issue of our times. We're destroying the planet and I don't think anyone, anywhere, can seriously get involved in politics without accepting some responsibility to try and stop the damage.'

Tom nodded in agreement. 'So what about the PAA? Isn't all of that what they're after, too?'

'I suppose so. But they're the lunatic fringe. They're driven by a sort of mad fanaticism that borders on hatred — quite of what, I don't know. Anyway, the word 'reason' doesn't seem to be part of their vocabulary. I don't think they really care about the issues so long as they have some outlet for their own violence.'

'So won't they blow it all for you?'

'Not if nobody makes the connection. And they'll get nailed sooner or later, anyway. They may be violent but you can bet they've never been through one of the Libyan training camps, like the pros. No, they're rank amateurs when it comes to terrorism.'

'So you just leave them to it?' Tom shook his head. 'You can't, Dad! They're still terrorists!'

'Christ, boy! How many times do I have to say it? I have *no choice*!'

For a moment Tom looked into the fire, collecting his thoughts, then said angrily: 'Yes you do, but you just can't face it. You can go to the police and admit you've been conned. Admit you're not perfect all the time. No one else expects you to be. I certainly don't.'

'But I do you, is that it?'

'Partly . . . yes . . . but that's not what we're talking about.

Go to the police! You've got to! Or maybe you just haven't got the guts?'

His father tensed momentarily, then slumped. He remained silent and pensive.

'Mum says you're a terrible idealist when it comes to politics,' said Tom more gently. 'I think your ideals are screwing you up.'

'Maybe so, son, maybe so,' said his father looking up and nodding.

'What are we going to tell Mr Davidson?' asked Christie nervously as they drew near to the cave.

'Exactly what we have in mind,' replied her grandmother tersely. 'I don't think he can possibly stop us. We'll be three against one.'

'But what if he's talked Tom round while we've been gone?'

'Then we'll just have to talk him back again. He's got a good deal more common sense than his father, that laddie.'

They ducked through the entrance and stepped into the cave. Tom and his father looked at them expectantly.

'We've found a boat,' announced Christie's grandmother, looking Bill Davidson straight in the eye. 'Christie and I are leaving. It's up to you whether you come with us, but don't you dare try and . . .'

'It's . . . er . . . all right.' He stood up, avoiding Christie's grandmother's gaze.

'Do I understand that you're coming with us, then?' asked Christie's grandmother, momentarily taken aback.

'Yes, Mrs McKenzie. I've done a little thinking and I've decided to . . . what was your expression . . . rearrange my priorities.'

'Well I'm very glad to hear it,' she replied, sounding not entirely convinced. 'We'd best get going in that case.'

They left the cave and headed inland, following an old sheep track across the southernmost tip of the island. The snow had let up for the time being and without the wind it was hard to imagine how they had had to battle their way down the shore the previous night.

She couldn't wait to get off Gruinard Island, Christie realised, as she led the way along the little path. It was perfectly safe, of course, and probably had been for some time; but there was, as Willie McLeod had said, a distinctly dead feel to the place. With its contours rising gradually to a low, rounded summit, it was not unlike a bloated brown corpse floating in Gruinard Bay. And thinking of corpses, what about the man in the snowstorm . . . ?

She dismissed the thought hastily and concentrated on the twists and turns of the sheep track which now led downhill towards a small bay, facing east to the mainland across a few hundred yards of leaden water.

At the far end of the shallow, sandy beach a buttress protruded from the cliff. Behind it a boulder-strewn gulley ran back into the cliff and at its furthest end was a dilapidated boathouse. Its doors were open and in the gloom within they could see the shape of a rowing boat.

'Amazing!' said Tom excitedly. 'How did you find it?'

'You tell him, Nan,' said Christie.

Her grandmother coughed, then explained: 'The shepherd used to row over from the mainland before the war, to see to the sheep. One spring there was a terrible storm when he was on the island. The boat was down at the old jetty there,' she pointed to a spine of boulders that ran into the water directly in front of the boathouse, 'and it was smashed to smithereens. He was marooned here for two days. So he persuaded the laird to build a boathouse and keep a spare here . . . just in case. I had a hunch that it might still be here. There was no reason for the biological people to remove it.'

The boat was clinker-built and heavy, its timber patchily bleached by the salt air where the varnish had peeled away. The rowlocks were pitted and red with rust and one of the thwarts was split. But thanks to the boathouse, it still retained a semblance of seaworthiness despite its shabby condition.

Tom and his father grasped it by the stern and began to heave it out towards the beach. They had reached the mouth of the gulley when Christie said:

'Wait a minute! Did you mean it when you said they'd be keeping an eye out for us, Mr Davidson?'

He gave her an uncomfortable look. 'I don't think they will really. I convinced them pretty well last night that we'd sit here and wait for them. But they hadn't bargained on your grandmother's powers of persuasion, or the fact that I'd brought my conscience along with me!' He glanced at Tom and laughed awkwardly. Tom blushed and heaved at the boat again.

It was not until they had the boat in the water and all four of them in it, that they realised how badly it was leaking. Little springs of water bubbled up between the floor timbers from stem to stern, forming puddles around their feet.

'What have we got to bail with?' asked Tom's father, removing the oars which lay undisturbed in the bottom and slotting them into the rowlocks.

'The thermos?' suggested Christie.

Tom's father glanced over his shoulder at the mainland, then shook his head. 'Not nearly enough. We'll only get across if I row like hell and you three bail as fast as you can. Tom, would you see what you can find on the beach?'

Tom scrambled from the boat and returned a couple of minutes later with a lidless kettle, a tin can and a plastic bottle. He pushed off and climbed back in again as his father bent to the oars and began to pull through the water, his strokes short and untidy at first, but lengthening as he found his rhythm.

As they began to glide over the still, dark water Christie became uncomfortably aware of their vulnerability: they were sitting ducks for anyone on the shore with a rifle. But soon the sheer physical effort of bailing drove all thought from her mind and by the time they reached the jetty below the woods of Gruinard House, twenty minutes later, her arms ached so much that she thought they must be about to come off. Despite her boots and thick socks, her feet had gone quite numb in the six inches of icy water that sloshed back and forth in the bottom of the boat.

Chrtistie's grandmother leaned back in the stern, gasping for breath. Bill Davidson slumped on the oars, his face scarlet and his forehead drenched with perspiration.

'It's too long since I last did that,' he panted.

For some minutes they sat in the boat, recovering their strength. Then they disembarked and walked up the jetty to the road.

'Shall we try the big house for a phone?' asked Christie.

'No, there's no one there at the moment,' her grandmother replied. 'We're best heading back for Laide and see if we can get a lift.'

'I wonder if anyone saw us?' Tom asked as they reached the tarmac.

'Does it matter, now?' asked Christie.

'No,' said Tom's father. 'Even if they were watching they wouldn't try anything on the main road, in broad daylight. We'll get to Laide, or Mellon Udrigle if we can, and ring the police straightaway. I think we've all had enough of this adventure.'

He gave a short, tense laugh and set off down the road.

Christie waited until he was some distance ahead, then asked: 'Is he really serious — about going to the police, I mean?'

'He seems to be,' said Tom, shivering at the chilling breeze which blew in off the bay.

'How did you get him to change his mind?'

'I told him that he does have a choice. And that he's a coward if he doesn't take it.' He paused, then continued: 'It's weird though. I can't figure him out. Maybe your nar was right — about him being confused. Alba Nova's terribly important to him, you know. I didn't realise before. And he seems to believe in important things . . .'

'Like what?'

'Like saving the planet. That's pretty important, I reckon.'

'Me too . . . So maybe he's not that bad after all?'

'Maybe.'

'D'you know what I think, Tom Davidson?'

'What?'

'I think you're brilliant!'

There was the sound of a vehicle approaching from behind. Christie's heartbeat quickened as she turned round. For all Tom's father's reassurances, she was not yet confident that they were out of danger. But she relaxed as she saw that it was a camper van with holiday stickers on its windows.

It slowed down and a man in a plaid shirt with red hair and an untidy red beard stuck his head out of the window.

'You folks need a lift?' He was English.

'That would be very kind,' said Christie's grandmother.

'I'm trying to find a place called Mellon something . . . Mellon Udrigle. Great name isn't it! That any good for you?'

'It's where we want to go,' said Christie.

'Terrific. Hop in then and you can show me the way. I hear they've got some holiday cabins there. I'm bringing the family up in the summer — we've got three kids now and this thing only sleeps four!'

Tom's father climbed into the front while Tom, Christie and her grandmother sat on the cross-facing seats in the back. The driver gave Tom's father a curious glance as he pulled off.

'If you don't mind my saying so, you look as if you've been out all night.'

Christie examined herself, then the others. He was right. Bill Davidson's chin had sprouted a thick stubble and his hair was matted and damp with perspiration. Her grandmother was pale. Strands of hair straggled untidily from under her headscarf and the corner of one eye had begun to twitch with exhaustion. Tom and she herself simply looked as if they'd slept in a ditch.

'No, no,' Bill Davidson answered smoothly. 'We just took the boat out earlier on this morning and ran out of fuel round in the mouth of Loch Broom, would you believe it! There's not much traffic on a Saturday at this time of year and we've had to walk a bit.'

'Quite a bit, by the look of it,' said the driver, raising an eyebrow.

'Yes. But we're used to doing things like this. Everyone's mad up here, you know!'

The driver laughed and began talking about the weather. Ten minutes later they reached Mellon Udrigle.

'Those are the cabins,' said Bill Davidson, pointing to the right. 'Just let us off here and we can walk the rest of the way.'

'OK,' said the driver, pulling to a halt. 'See you later. And good luck with the boat!'

They thanked him and climbed out.

'Do you not want to go to your cabin?' asked Christie's grandmother as they walked towards the cottages.

Bill Davidson shook his head. 'I don't want to get involved in a long conversation about letting arrangements and so on. We've got more important things to do. I'll go over later, once he's gone.'

They reached the cottage. An ancient Volvo estate car was parked outside.

'Whose is that?' asked Bill Davidson.

'My neighbour's — Neil Cameron,' said Christie's grandmother.

'Is he around?'

'I don't know. He could be in the house. He could be out with his sheep. Why do you ask?'

'I'd rather we didn't have to start explaining things yet. Come on, let's get inside.'

Once indoors, Christie's grandmother made straight for the telephone in the living room, without stopping even to remove her coat. Bill Davidson followed her in. As she was about to dial, he said quietly: 'Perhaps I should make this call.'

She turned round, receiver in hand, and looked at him.

'It is really my responsibility,' he continued. 'I'm to blame, aren't I?' His face flickered with a smile which Christie's grandmother did not return.

'As you wish,' she said coolly, putting down the receiver. 'The number's there. You want Sergeant Drummond. I'll get us something decent to eat.' She made to leave the room.

'Wait a minute.' He was looking down at the phone number. 'This is Ullapool, isn't it?'

She nodded.

'It's at least an hour's drive from here. Why not Aultbea, or Gairloch?'

'Because Sergeant Drummond's the senior officer in the area. They're only constables in Aultbea and Gairloch and they'd just get in touch with him in any case. It's quicker to go direct. And I know Drummond's in regular contact with the CID in Inverness because of all the Russian fishing boats that are in and out of Ullapool.'

'Oh. All right.'

In the kitchen Tom filled up the stove, which had almost gone out, while Christie and her grandmother prepared sausages, bacon, eggs and toast.

Tom's father's voice drifted through from the living room. Then there was a 'ting' as the receiver went down and he appeared in the kitchen.

'Well,' he said with an air of finality. 'That's that. We can all relax now. Drummond's on his way.'

'And a good thing, too,' muttered Christie's grandmother from the stove.

When the food was ready they ate ravenously and in silence. The drama might be over, thought Christie, but there was still a tension round the table. Bill Davidson seemed to be avoiding Tom's eye and her grandmother gazed steadfastly at her plate, a tiny tremor in her hands as she ate.

'Why did Dougal Mackay have to hide the explosives in *Loch na Beiste*?' she asked of no one in particular, hoping to lighten the atmosphere.

'I expect because Ross's place was too obvious,' replied Tom's father. 'A quarry's the first place you'd go to if you were looking for explosives.'

'But why particularly *Loch na Beiste*?'

'I don't know,' he shrugged. 'Perhaps it's the least conspicuous of the lochs on his round.'

'Not inconspicuous enough, fortunately,' added Christie's grandmother without raising her eyes.

'And what about the fuel depot?' Christie continued. 'Why did they choose that . . . I mean . . . apart from it being an easy target?'

'Because there's no such thing as a Scottish navy,' Bill Davidson replied, wiping his plate clean with a corner of toast. 'The fuel dump's a symbol of English rule. And it'll make a big bang. They'll get a lot of coverage out of it.'

'Would have done,' Tom corrected him.

His father gave a short laugh. 'Sorry, would have done.' He pushed back his chair and rose. 'That was very good. Thank you, Mrs McKenzie, Christie. Now, if you'll excuse me, I'll get over to the cabin for a while before Drummond arrives. I want to get out of these clothes and have a shave. You staying, Tom?'

Tom nodded.

'See you shortly, then.'

Christie's grandmother's face relaxed visibly as he left the room.

An hour later Tom, Christie and her grandmother remained at the kitchen table, chatting.

'Sergeant Drummond should be here by now,' said Christie's grandmother with a note of impatience.

Christie glanced at the clock on the dresser. Four-thirty.

Time seemed out of joint. They must have left the cave around one o'clock, but it could have been an hour ago — or a day. Despite the long sleep she felt fidgety and charged with tiredness.

'Why don't you ring again, Nan? Make sure he's on his way.'

'Yes, I think I will.' She rose from the table and was halfway across the room when they heard the front door opening and Neil Cameron's voice booming down the hall:

'Anyone in?'

'In the kitchen, Neil,' Christie's grandmother called out.

Neil Cameron entered, a look of outrage on his face.

'So you are here, after all! I thought you'd gone away. Anyway, some so-and-so's just driven off in my car. Of all the bloody cheek! Drove away in broad daylight. You didn't see anyone, did you?'

'No,' Christie replied. 'We've been in here all the . . .'

'Wait a minute!' Tom leapt to his feet, pushed past Neil and fled from the roon.

'What's going on?' asked Neil, his expression changing to one of perplexity.

'We'll find out in a minute,' said Christie's grandmother. 'He's off to the cabin, I don't doubt.'

'I'd better call the police, then,' said Neil, recovering himself.

'Just wait, Neil. Wait till the lad's back.' Christie's grandmother motioned him to sit down. 'We've been having a spot of trouble too,' she added in response to his quizzically cocked eyebrow.

A few minutes later Tom returned, flushed and out of breath. 'He's gone! Vanished!'

'Who's gone?' asked Neil, beginning to sound irritated. 'Will someone please tell me what's going on?'

'My dad,' said Tom. 'It was probably him in your car.' He turned to Christie and her grandmother with a despairing look. 'And I bet he didn't really call the police.'

'But why?' asked Christie. 'What on earth could he be up to?'

'God knows. I think he must've lost his . . .'

Christie's grandmother raised her arms for silence. 'All right, all right, we'll go into that later. First, I think we should explain to Neil what's been going on. Then we'll call Sergeant Drummond.'

Neil Cameron's brow furrowed in deepening horror as, between them, they related the events of the last twenty-four hours.

'Right,' he said decisively, when they were done. 'This has got to stop, and quick. Where's your phone, Eileen?'

'In the sitting room.'

'OK.' He left the room.

Tom slumped at the table, his head in his hands. 'I really thought he meant it, you know. I thought that I'd actually got through to him. Seems I was wrong. I shouldn't think I ever will.' His voice was sharp with bitterness and frustration.

'We don't know that you didn't, yet, Tom,' said Christie's grandmother gently.

Neil re-appeared in the kitchen, his hands spread incomprehendingly. 'It's dead. The phone's dead.'

'Well it worked an hour ago,' said Christie. 'At least it pinged when he put the receiver down, even if he didn't make the call.'

'Try yours, Neil,' suggested her grandmother.

Neil disappeared next door and returned shortly, shaking his head. 'He must've pulled down the wires. It wouldn't be difficult. They come in behind the cabins. The poles are low. A good swipe with a long branch would do it.'

'But why?' muttered Tom wretchedly. 'What the hell's he up to?'

'Stopping us contacting the police, I imagine,' said Christie's grandmother sourly. 'Or at least delaying us.'

'What for?'

'There's only two possible reasons from what you've told

me,' said Neil thoughtfully. 'Either he's in cahoots with them and he's been kidding you all along, or he's gone off to try and stop them on his own.'

'But why should he do that?' Christie asked.

The question hung in the air as they all looked at one another in silence. Then Tom said slowly: 'I think I know.' The idea seemed still to be forming as he spoke. 'Because that way he can . . . you know . . . save face. If he goes after them alone he'll be a hero and people won't think badly of him for being conned by them in the first place. You see, he's terrified of losing Alba Nova . . .'

'But that's crazy!' said Christie. 'There's one of him against three of them, at the least, and they've got guns and explosives and heaven knows what else.'

'He used to be a Royal Marine,' said Tom without much conviction.

'Royal Marine! Pah!' said her grandmother angrily. 'It's more than crazy. It's totally irresponsible — to leave us here without protection while he swans off like some . . . some mad mediaeval knight.'

Tom nodded miserably. 'It's my fault, you know. I called him a coward. I should've known.'

'Nonsense, laddie!' Christie's grandmother retorted. 'If it hadn't been for you we'd still be on Gruinard Island. And anyway, we don't know for certain what he's doing. We can only guess. Now, what are *we* to do?' She looked to Neil for guidance.

'I think one of us should get up to Laide immediately and phone Drummond,' he replied. 'It had better be me, just in case they're on the prowl. I'm the only one they don't know.'

Christie's grandmother nodded in agreement. 'Have you any other way of getting there?'

'No, I had an old bike, but I got rid of it.'

'There's mine,' said Christie hesitantly, 'but I think it would be a bit small.'

'I think so,' said Neil with a grimace. 'Well, it'll just have to be Shank's pony, then. It'll take me three-quarters of an hour. I'll borrow Janet's car and come back for you as soon as I've rung. It would be safer to wait for Drummond at the post office than here.' He glanced at his watch. 'It's coming up for five now, so I should be back by six. Meanwhile, I think you should go into my house — and make sure the doors are locked. OK?'

This was not the way things should be going, thought Christie nervously as she followed Tom and her grandmother into Neil's cottage.

Not the way at all.

Chapter 11

Bill Davidson had his foot hard down, pushing the old Volvo for every ounce of speed she would give him. He came fast down the hill towards Aultbea and swung south, following the main road to Gairloch.

Up on his left, poking out from behind the corner of the wood, were the tiers of the fuel tanks. Below him, to the right, were the circular humps of the valve and pump stations and further down still, the gantry-crowned jetty. He glanced briefly up the hill, then down to the shore but there was no sign of life. He hadn't really expected any. They wouldn't be there till after dark.

He pressed on, the deserted road climbing and dipping as it wound along the shore of Loch Ewe. This dismal weather must be keeping people indoors, he thought gratefully, as he sped past the Inverewe Gardens car park where a handful of bedraggled tourists waited patiently beside their solitary bus in an acre of empty tarmac.

Once through the village of Poolewe, the road turned inland and climbed gently along the bank of the River Ewe towards Loch Maree. The snow had started to fall again. He switched on the windscreen wipers and peered out, anxiously scanning the right-hand verge. A wood loomed ahead and there, amongst the twisted Caledonian pines, was what he had been looking for — a track, leading off into the trees. At its foot was a faded sign: Ross Quarries Ltd. No Trespassing. No Liability.

A quarter of a mile further on was a lay-by. He parked the car, got out and walked back towards the wood, pulling up the hood of his waterproof as he went.

The track was heavily rutted and muddy with melted snow. It wound up through the trees for two or three hundred yards before emerging on the shoulder of a hill around which it curled, still climbing.

As he came out of the trees he paused for a moment, then stepped off the track and headed across the heather, making for the opposite shoulder. Ten minutes later he dropped to the ground and wormed his way up the final few yards to the brow of the hill on his stomach. He peered over and grunted in satisfaction at what he saw, his breath clouding in the chill, damp air.

Directly beneath him, as if someone had taken a huge bite out of the hillside, the semi-circular face of the quarry fell a hundred feet or more to an uneven floor, strewn with snow-sprinkled piles of gravel and large, purposeful-looking pieces of machinery. At the quarry's mouth was a Porta-kabin, its light on and figures dimly visible through steamed-up windows. Parked beside it was a white Gàirloch Salmon landrover. But where the devil were the other vehicles?

He dropped back below the brow and set off again around the far side of the hill. The snow was coming more heavily now, veering to the horizontal on a rising wind. Blinking constantly as he walked, he almost fell into the secondary quarry before he saw it. It was a good deal smaller than the main one and more horseshoe-shaped with a correspond-ingly narrower entrance, across which was parked a large gravel-truck. He could just pick out the word 'Ross' on the muddy cab door.

Behind the truck, and concealed from the view of anyone

passing by the quarry-mouth, were his own Range Rover, Christie's grandmother's small saloon and Ross's grey estate car. A couple of tarpaulins had been thrown over them for good measure.

He descended cautiously, pausing for a moment by a large sign at the entrance which read DANGER – BLASTING, to check that no one was coming up the track from the main quarry. Then he climbed into the cab of the gravel-truck and felt beneath the steering wheel. His hand closed on a bundle of cables and he yanked hard. There was a satisfying ripping sound as they came away.

He dismounted from the truck and glanced past it to the tarpaulin-shrouded cars. Better do the job properly. He lifted an edge of the canvas and opened the door of the first. It was Ross's. The canvas fell back as the door swung to, casting the interior of the car into semi-darkness. He felt inside his coat and produced a large flashlight which he played beneath the steering column. There. He wrenched and the wires fell free.

Christie's grandmother's car was sandwiched so tightly between the other two that it would clearly be impossible to open the doors. It would have to be a tyre job on that one. He moved round to the Range Rover, climbed in and, with a brief grimace at the irony of being forced to vandalise his own hard-earned property, grabbed the cables and disabled the ignition. Finally he slashed the tyres on Christie's grandmother's car with a penknife.

Now the landrover. That might be a little trickier. But he was beginning to enjoy himself: the adrenalin was racing nicely, bringing back memories of night exercises, all those years ago. He'd forgotten how exhilarating it was — better even than pulling off a business deal. Maybe he'd take some of the Alba Nova committee on one of those executive adventure weekends once all this was over. That would sharpen them up.

He dropped down below the track and followed it back to the mouth of the main quarry, then peered cautiously over the bank. The light still burned in the office and no one was about. He scrambled up the bank, sprinted across the track and ducked down in the lee of the Portakabin. Its occupant's voices were faintly audible. He eased himself erect and glanced briefly through the corner of the nearest window. Good. All three of them were there, seated round the table on which were spread what he took to be the contents of the diver's bag.

He dropped down again and ran at a crouch to the landrover, slipping round to the side facing away from the Portakabin.

He began slowly to open the door, unaware as he did so that an immense, heavily-bearded man in a boiler suit had slid from the shadows on the other side of the quarry and was moving silently towards the landrover, hefting a length of metal pipe in one hand as he advanced.

In Neil Cameron's cluttered sitting room, Tom and Christie sat over a draughts board by the unlit fire. Christie's grandmother stood at the shabby lace curtains, staring out towards the road.

A fine veil of wet snow, almost sleet, fell across the bay. Although it was only five-thirty, the light was as poor as on a November afternoon.

Christie moved her man and Tom deliberated longer than necessary before taking him, along with two others. Neither of them were concentrating properly. Christie felt fogged with anxiety and exhaustion. Tom had reverted to his old posture: shoulders drooping and head hung.

Christie's grandmother straightened at the window. 'Here's Kenny Tulloch,' she announced, sounding a little surprised. 'I wonder what brings him here on a Saturday afternoon? He's driving very fast.'

Christie scrambled to her feet, knocking over the draughts board, and dashed to the window. The Gairloch Salmon landrover was speeding down the hill towards the beach . . . turning right towards the cabins . . .

'It's not Kenny!' she cried, grabbing her startled grandmother by the sleeve and pulling her away from the window. 'It's Dougal Mackay! Quick, we must hide! He's bound to come here when he finds the cabin's empty.'

'Upstairs!' said Tom. 'Into one of the bedrooms!'

They fled upstairs and entered Neil's bedroom. Tom stopped, his eye caught by the trapdoor in the low cottage ceiling. He glanced quickly around the room. A pair of folding steps were stacked down the side of the wardrobe.

'Into the loft!' he whispered. 'It's the safest place.'

He removed the steps and set them up beneath the trapdoor, climbed up and eased back the square wooden inset. Then he heaved himself into the hole, turned round and lowered his arms.

'Come on, Mrs McKenzie.'

Christie's grandmother ascended the steps and reached up for Tom's arms. Tom pulled, Christie shoved as best she could from below and her grandmother scrabbled her way, gasping, into the loft.

As Christie followed them up into the darkness there was a screech of brakes outside, then the sound of doors slamming and voices going up the path to her grandmother's cottage. Christie turned round to close the trapdoor behind her and glanced down into the room.

'Tom!' she whispered. 'They'll see the steps!'

Tom lowered himself again, replaced the steps by the wardrobe and jumped for the edge of the hole. He fell short and landed with a thud. For a moment they froze. The voices were still audible but muted now as they moved about next door.

Tom jumped again and this time his fingers closed on the rim of the trap. Christie grabbed his wrists and hauled with all her might. His head appeared, then his shoulders. He hooked his elbows over the edge and pulled himself in. Christie closed the trapdoor behind him.

'You know what this means,' whispered Tom, his voice shaking. 'They've got Dad.'

'As long as they haven't got Neil, too . . .' panted Christie's grandmother.

'We did lock the doors, didn't we?' asked Christie nervously.

'Yes,' said Tom.

Although it was almost pitch dark where they sat, at the opposite end of the loft a grubby, cobwebbed skylight admitted a meagre shaft of grey gloom. Tom rose and tiptoed towards it, a dark silhouette dodging unseen obstacles.

As he peered through the dirty glass, the door slammed next door and the voices grew louder. He remained at the skylight for only a few moments, then returned stealthily to the trapdoor.

'It's Mackay,' he whispered, 'and he's brought a gorilla with him.'

'Gorilla?' queried Christie's grandmother.

'Yes, a huge guy in a boiler suit and a woolly hat.'

There was a moment's silence, then Christie's grandmother asked: 'Has he a great big beard?'

'Yes . . . yes, I think so.'

'That'll be Wee Hughie Soutar — Ross's chief quarry-hand. He's none too bright and he has a dreadful temper on him . . .'

'They must be here somewhere.' It was Mackay's voice, coming up the garden path. 'Davidson came on his own. I'm sure he won't have involved anyone else yet. He'll have them hidden away, waiting for him. I'd lay money on it.'

The front door handle rattled impatiently, then stopped. There was a pause, then a deep, slow voice said:

'Will I give it the shoulder, Dougal?'

'Aye, might as well.'

There was a splintering crash and heavy footfalls echoed through the hallway. Christie reached involuntarily for Tom's hand.

'You check upstairs, Hughie. I'll look down here.'

The stairs creaked beneath ponderous, uneven footsteps

which stopped for a second on the landing, then went into the other bedroom. They came out again, the bathroom door opened and closed and then the handle to Neil's bedroom door turned.

Christie shrank back from the edge of the trap, sensing Tom and her grandmother do likewise as the footsteps clumped slowly around the room, then halted directly beneath them. Her mouth was dry and her heart beat wildly. She gripped Tom's hand as tightly as she could. It was damp with sweat.

The seconds passed and she was beginning to fear she might explode with tension when Mackay's voice carried up the stairs: 'Anything there, Hughie?'

The feet moved beneath them and the voice boomed in reply: 'No. Not so far. But there's the loft yet.'

There was another long silence, then Mackay said: 'I wouldn't bother. They'd never've got the old biddy up there. Come on, we're wasting our time.'

Hughie thumped out of the room and down the stairs. He paused at the front door: 'Where'll we look now, Dougal?'

'Nowhere. We're best to get back and keep our fingers crossed that they just stay put wherever they are for another few hours. It won't matter after that.'

'Why not?'

'Because Davidson won't allow them to breathe a word once Bertie's finished with him. You know Bertie. He likes to have a . . . wee chat . . . with people.'

Hughie laughed unpleasantly and the footsteps retreated down the garden path. Shortly the landrover started up, then pulled away. The noise of the engine dwindled and a minute later there was silence.

'Old biddy, indeed!' muttered Christie's grandmother, letting out her breath. 'Still, I suppose it saved us.'

'Let's get out of here,' said Christie, sliding back the trapdoor. Like the cave, the darkened loft was beginning to make her feel claustrophobic.

'No,' said Tom. 'I think we should wait for Neil to come back. Just in case . . .'

'That would be sensible,' agreed Christie's grandmother. 'He shouldn't be too long now . . . if all's well.'

Christie took a deep breath and settled back in the darkness. She felt Tom's arm creep slowly round her shoulder, more confidently this time, and allowed her head to tilt back against it. It was a good feeling; at the same time reassuring and . . . something else she couldn't quite describe.

Ten minutes later there was the sound of a vehicle approaching. It halted abruptly outside the cottage.

Tom kicked the trapdoor back into place with his foot and scrambled hastily along to the skylight. For a tense moment he peered through in silence, then called out jubilantly: 'It's OK. It's Neil.'

Christie opened the trapdoor again as Tom returned and he lowered himself through it, dropping to the floor.

'We're in the bedroom!' he called out, moving across to fetch the steps.

As Christie clambered down, Neil burst into the room.

'Thank God!' he exclaimed, glancing at the steps then up at the trapdoor. 'Are you all right up there, Eileen?' he called.

'I've been worse, thank you, Neil,' came the muffled reply as a pair of brogue-shod feet appeared in the cavity. Woollen-stockinged legs followed and with a good deal of help from Tom and Neil, Christie's grandmother descended from the loft.

'We've had visitors,' she said, standing up and straightening her clothes.

'So I see,' Neil replied. 'The same two that've nearly just driven me off the road in Kenny Tulloch's landrover, I suppose . . .' he raised a hand to stem their alarm, '. . . it's all right, they were going much too fast to see me, and anyway, they wouldn't know Janet's car. I guess it was Mackay driving, but who was the other one?'

'Wee Hughie Soutar — from Ross's quarry.'

Neil raised an eyebrow. 'Wee Hughie, eh? That would explain the state of my front door, then.'

'They've got my father,' said Tom flatly.

'I thought as much,' said Neil. 'But there's nothing we can do now till Drummond arrives. It won't be long.' His face brightened as he added: 'He was like a cat on a hot tin roof when I told him what's been happening! Every bobby in the county'll be here within an hour, not to mention the chopper squad from Inverness.'

'But we don't know where they are,' said Tom.

'It can't be far away if Mackay was down here so qui . . .'

'Neil, have you got another of those?' It was Christie. Her voice was shaking and the colour had drained from her face as she pointed to the bedside table where, next to the alarm clock, sat a large yellow flashlight.

'There's a clock in the kitchen . . .'

'No, no. Not the clock, the flashlight!'

'Yes, as a matter of fact I do. I keep it in the car. Why?'

All three of them were now looking at her curiously.

Christie ignored Neil's question. She felt a flutter of panic as the dragon stirred, but she couldn't stop now.

'Tom,' she asked slowly, 'what colour's the lining of your dad's waterproof?'

'Wha . . . what's that got to do with anything?'

'Just tell me!' she said fiercely. 'What colour is it?'

Her urgency was beginning to communicate itself to the others. Neil and her grandmother regarded her intently as Tom searched his memory.

'Tartan, I'm pretty sure,' he said at length.

'Oh no!' said Christie, almost to herself. 'It was *him*!' She sat down heavily on the bed.

There was a moment's silence, then a babel of questions:

'Who?'

'What d'you mean?'

'What are you talking about?'

'What's happening, Christie?'

When she looked up her eyes were glazed and her voice distant: 'I know what's going to happen to Tom's dad.' She turned slowly to glance through the window at the late afternoon light and nodded to herself. 'It hasn't happened yet. But it won't be long.'

'How do you know . . . ?' Neil began, but Christie's grandmother motioned him to silence as Tom exclaimed softly: 'The cave! What you saw . . . in the fire!'

Christie nodded. Her head dropped to her hands and she began to sob violently.

Tom sat down beside her and put his arm around her, but she shrugged him away so he stood up again and hovered in the centre of the room, uncertain what to do with himself. Christie's grandmother meanwhile had pulled Neil into a corner and was whispering to him. Neil glanced across at Christie as she spoke, his features at first widening in disbelief, then gradually softening with a mixture of sympathy and respect.

When she had finished, her grandmother moved over to the bed and squatted down beside it, taking both her granddaughter's hands in hers.

'Christie, dear, can you tell us what you saw?' she asked gently.

Christie looked up, her face tear-stained. 'I saw a man running across the hill,' she began haltingly. 'It was snowing and the light was going. I couldn't see his face. I knew he was being chased. He was afraid. I could feel it. Anyway, he tripped and a yellow flashlight fell out of his poacher's pocket . . .' She paused and wiped her eyes on her sleeve.

'Go on, dear,' encouraged her grandmother.

'He ran up a hill towards a cliff, or a big bank. When he got to the top he heard something and turned round. Then there was a noise like a gun going off and he fell . . . over the cliff.'

'Oh, Jesus!' said Tom, as the full implication dawned. 'Are you quite sure it was my dad?' His eyes were wide with horror.

'Well . . . I never saw his face. But the flashlight and the tartan coat-lining . . . yes, I'm sure of it.'

There was a moment's silence, Then Neil asked: 'Do you have any idea where it was, Christie?'

'Somewhere on the hill, but I don't know where. It could've been any hill, I suppose.'

'Was there anything you'd recognise?' Neil persisted. 'A road, a loch maybe, big stones, anything distinctive?'

'Yes,' she replied slowly. 'There was. There was a huge boulder at the edge of the cliff. It had a face on it like an ugly old woman — with a hook nose and a pointed chin.'

Neil thought for a moment, then exclaimed: '*Morag Dubh*! Black Morag! She was burned in 1712 for bewitching cattle in Poolewe. There's a big stone named after her up on the hill between Poolewe and Loch Maree. Come to think of it, it's only about a mile from Ross's quarry. Of course! That's where they'll be!' He thumped the end of the bed with his fist. 'Come on, we'd better get up to the post office to meet Drummond.'

'No!' Christie stood up and glared at him defiantly, her eyes large and bright in the pale oval of her face. 'It may be too late by the time he arrives. We must go there ourselves.'

'But Christie,' said her grandmother, 'they're armed . . . probably desperate . . . what can we do?'

'That's what I've got to find out, Nan. Don't you see?' Her voice was rising, trembling. 'I've got to find out if I *can* do anything . . . if I'm *supposed* to do anything . . . to change what I see. Maybe not . . . maybe I can't but I *must* know. You've got to understand . . . !' She turned away and moved to the window, her shoulders quivering.

Neil and her grandmother exchanged glances. Tom stood by, his long fingers drumming nervously against his thighs.

After a while her grandmother walked over to her and put a hand on her arm. 'Christie, dear, there may be other chances . . . less dangerous . . .'

Christie spun round, her eyes blurred with tears. 'No, Nan! I couldn't bear it again without knowing. It has to be this time!' She turned to the window again.

Her grandmother spread her hands helplessly and looked at Neil and Tom. 'What am I to say, then? I know how important it is . . . I understand how she must be feeling . . . but her parents . . . I'd never forgive myself . . . and there's you too, Tom . . . we must think about this a minute . . .'

'Wait . . .' It was Tom, a look of intensity on his pale face. 'Mr Cameron, what about this *Morag Dubh*? Do you know the place?'

Neil nodded to himself. 'When I was a lad I used to take . . . well, no matter. Yes, I do know it quite well.'

'Then assuming Christie's right, assuming he's managed to escape and is running near the stone, out in the open, is there anywhere we could see it but not be seen . . . remain invisible, so to speak?'

Neil thought for a moment, then said: 'There's the big wood. The track to the quarry goes up through the far end. I suppose at the downhill end, nearer Poolewe, the top of the wood would be about two hundred yards from the stone. You could hide in the trees at the edge and not be seen, yes.'

'And could we create some kind of a diversion, d'you think, without putting ourselves in danger?'

Neil looked at him doubtfully. 'This is pretty serious, what you're suggesting.'

'It's a serious situation.' Tom glanced pointedly at Christie; then, without changing his inflection, added: 'We could be talking about my dad's life.'

'That we could,' Neil agreed.

'Do you have a gun?'

'Yes, I've an old 12-bore. Haven't used it in years.'

'Maybe if we let off shots in the wood at the right moment?' Tom suggested.

'Maybe. I don't like it much, though.'

'Me neither . . . but look . . . we're not talking about actually confronting them, or even getting anywhere close to them . . . and we've *got* to do something. How about if Christie and Mrs McKenzie wait at the roadside in the car and you and I go up to the wood. Then if anything goes wrong we can leg it back to the road. There aren't that many of them and if their base is the quarry they're unlikely to be lurking about in the wood.'

'We-ell . . .' Neil looked reluctant.

'Mrs McKenzie, what d'you think? Would you be prepared to wait for us in the car? I'm sure you'd be quite safe on the road . . . with the engine running . . .'

Christie's grandmother appeared to be wrestling with her conscience.

'I suppose . . .' she began but Christie turned round imploringly: 'Please, Nan, please! We . . . I . . . I've got to . . .'

'All right,' she said decisively. 'But you and I stay put in the car. We leave a message at Janet's telling Drummond exactly where we are and we pray that he gets there before anything happens. Neil . . . ?'

He glanced at Christie and gave a brief smile. 'OK.'

A quarter of an hour later Christie's grandmother emerged from the post office.

'Right, that's all sorted out with Janet,' she said briskly as she closed the car door. 'Let's get going.'

They drove off. Christie sat in the back next to Tom who was cradling the old shotgun on his knee. No one spoke.

Were they crazy, Christie wondered, to be pitting themselves against a bunch of armed terrorists? Yes, they were. But then everything that had happened in the last few days had been crazy. Reality had slipped some time ago, she realised, as she gazed out at the louring, cloud-covered hills and the sullen, metallic water; the snow, flurrying across the windscreen, served only to increase her sense of inhabiting some strange half-world where nothing was quite as she knew it.

The one certainty in this almost-dream, indeed the only thing now that kept her going in the face of emotional and physical exhaustion, was her desperate need for confirmation: either way, it didn't seem to matter which, any longer. Just as long as she knew for sure, then she could deal with it better in the future.

It was almost, she thought with a shiver, as if she were being driven to discover the colour of the dragon's eyes.

'We'll be there in a couple of minutes,' said Neil tersely as they pulled out of Poolewe and began the gentle ascent towards Loch Maree.

'Did you remember the cartridges?' asked Tom. His voice sounded thin and nervous.

There was a dull rattle as Neil patted his left-hand pocket.

Shortly the wood appeared on their right, looming darkly in the grey light. Neil followed its length, looking for somewhere to park, but there was nowhere apart from the quarry track.

'Damn it!' he muttered. 'I should've stopped in the lay-by back there.'

'You can turn in the next one,' said Christie's grand-mother quietly. 'It's not far.'

As they approached the second lay-by Neil gave a grunt of surprise. 'Well, well! He's at the quarry all right. There's my car. Look!'

He pulled off the road and stopped, then jumped out leaving the engine running. 'I'll just be a minute,' he called over his shoulder.

Less than a minute later he was back. He lowered himself into the driver's seat, turned to Christie and nodded.

'You're right,' he said. 'The flashlight's gone.'

Chapter 12

'Good luck!' said Christie's grandmother softly as Neil got out of the car. She also got out and moved round to take her place behind the wheel.

Christie caught Tom's eye as he scrambled from the back seat, but she said nothing. He gave her arm a brief squeeze.

The lower end of the wood was no more than a hundred yards up the road from the first lay-by. Neil, nonetheless, was cautious.

'We don't want to get arrested with this thing before we've even begun,' he said, taking the gun from Tom.

He checked for approaching vehicles, then sprinted across the road, clambered over a stone dyke and ducked down in the field the other side. Tom followed him. A soggy-looking highland cow regarded them curiously for a moment then lowered its head in disinterest.

Keeping low, they made their way quickly through the field to the wood and once in its shelter, began to climb, for the trees rose steeply from the roadside. In the twilight gloom of the wood they had to concentrate hard where they were putting their feet. Neil swore sofly as he tripped against a fallen branch. There was a sudden movement in the undergrowth off to their left and they both stopped dead. A moment later a sheep ambled into view, trailing a creeper of bramble from its coat. They set off again.

Five minutes later they paused, out of breath, within twenty yards of the edge of the wood. Neil put a finger to his lips and motioned Tom to stay where he was. Then he crept forward until he was behind one of the outermost trees and peered cautiously to left and right. After a while he signalled to Tom to join him.

The light was now beginning to fail and with the continuous drift of snowflakes across the landscape, the features of the place were becoming less distinct every minute.

'There's the quarry,' said Neil softly, pointing to the dim silhouette of a hump-backed hill, half a mile to their left. His outstretched finger traced a line across the bleak expanse of undulating, snow-speckled heather before them. 'And there's Morag.'

Directly ahead, a couple of hundred yards off, the face of the old crone scowled malevolently on the crest of an escarpment, a light covering of snow on her head lending the incongruous impression of a lace cap. In the intervening space the ground climbed and dipped, then climbed again, obscuring all but the first few feet of the precipitous drop beyond the stone.

After a while Neil turned away and moved in behind the tree again, facing back into the wood. He pulled two cartridges from his pocket, slipped them into the breech of the gun and snapped it shut.

'I'll stay here,' he said. 'We should get a nice boom if I fire into the trees. You keep look-out and tell me when things start happening. OK?'

'OK,' said Tom.

'Right, let's get into position — and be ready to run like hell as soon as I've fired.'

Tom took his place behind a neighbouring tree, edging around the trunk until he had a clear view of the ground ahead.

He could feel the chill air beginning to bite through his clothes as he settled down to wait. But there was a deeper, more pervasive chill spreading through him as he found his gaze drawn to and held fast by the grotesque profile of *Morag Dubh*.

Bill Davidson opened his eyes and closed them again immediately. The light sent needles into his already-pounding head. There were other needles somewhere else. He conducted a mental search of his body for the source of the pain. There — his neck and shoulders. Aahh! and that wasn't all. His ribs. Oh God, they hurt too. Someone had really done him over.

The ringing in his ears was beginning to subside. Voices took its place. He opened his eyes again, slowly, and looked around.

He was on the floor in the Portakabin, his head jammed into a corner, his hips wedged between a filing cabinet and an ancient armchair. Through the gap he could see the flicker of a paraffin stove and beyond it, legs arranged round a table.

It was beginning to come back to him: the explosion in the back of his head when he was half-in, half-out of the landrover; then recovering consciousness, only to be set upon by Ross junior who had beaten him ferociously about the ribs while Ross senior stood by hurling abuse. He had passed out again . . .

'Aha! The sleeping beauty awakes.' Bertie Ross's voice cut through the chatter at the table. A chair scraped back and Ross was standing over him.

'Had a nice rest?'

Bill Davidson said nothing.

'So we've lost our tongue! Good. That'll do just fine.'

'Si-i-lent night, si-i-lent night . . .' Ross junior began to sing, off-key.

'Cut it out, Kevin!' said Dougal Mackay, laughing harshly as he rose from the table. 'Come on, the light's going. I think it's time we made a move.'

Bill Davidson tried to sit up but Ross prodded him in the chest with one foot and he fell back again.

'You just stay there now, nice and relaxed. We've a little business to attend to. You may even hear it if you listen hard.' He grinned as he added: 'We'll be leaving Hughie to look after you.'

He turned away and addressed the other end of the room: 'You'll be attentive to Mr Davidson's needs, won't you, Hughie?'

'Oh, I will, Bertie. I surely will,' came the reply. It was followed by the click of a rifle bolt being slid into place.

'Are we ready, then?' said Mackay. He sounded tense.

'Yes,' Kevin replied.

'OK. One last check, Kevin. Bolt cutters?'

'Yes,'

'Explosive?'

'Yes.'

'Detonators?'

'Yes.'

'Ignition?'

'Yes.'

'Timers?'

'Yes.'

'Masks and gloves?'

'Yes.'

'Right. Let's go.'

They left the Portakabin and the door closed behind them. Bill Davidson waited for the sound of the landrover starting up. But it did not come and instead he heard their voices dwindle as they walked out of the quarry and down the track.

It took a moment or two for the realisation to dawn that they were going to Aultbea on foot. It was, of course, by far the most obvious thing for them to do. Once they had crossed the river it was about six miles over the hill; they would be seen by no one and they would approach the fuel dump, in darkness, from the high ground behind it. They had never needed the vehicles in the first place.

He lay still and ground his teeth, partly in pain, partly in shame at his own stupidity. He would never have lived this down in the Marines. And the police were bound to be on their way by now. Mackay and the big fellow had failed to find Mrs McKenzie and the kids and there was no doubt in his mind that the obstinate old woman would have managed to get herself, by hook or by crook, to a phone.

Well, there was only one thing left to do now if he was to have any chance of redeeming himself — escape.

He hauled himself slowly into the sitting position and looked around. Hughie had pulled a chair in front of the door and sat with the rifle at the slant across his chest. He scowled menacingly and lowered the rifle as his captive's head appeared over the armchair.

'Going somewhere?'

'No, no,' Bill Davidson grunted, his eye falling on the paraffin stove. It was of the old design, cylindrical like a chimney, and portable. It sat somewhat insecurely on a couple of bricks, only a few inches from his right foot.

He gave an exaggerated groan, closed his eyes and lay back again, thinking hard.

Ten minutes later he shifted position, as if in sleep, and eased his body an inch or two further down the floor towards the stove. He heard Hughie's footsteps approaching across the floor and halting. He sensed that he was being inspected and gave what he hoped was a convincingly somnolent sigh. The footsteps retreated.

He waited a further ten minutes to give Hughie time to relax and to be certain that the others would be well on their way. Then he took a deep breath and shifted again on the floor, lazily stretching out his right foot until he felt it make contact with the base of the stove. Gently he increased the pressure with his foot until the stove began to yield, then he gave a swift, powerful push.

He heard the stove topple and crash to the ground,

immediately followed by a *whumph* of flame, then a crackle and a sharp singeing smell as the upholstery of the armchair caught. There was a startled oath from Hughie who came pounding across the room.

He remained inert until nearby flailing noises told him that his gaoler was fully occupied in trying to extinguish the blaze. Then he scrambled to his feet and barged forward, catching the startled Hughie, who was bent over the armchair, a hefty blow in the midriff with his elbow.

Hughie grunted and staggered backwards as Bill Davidson dodged past him, sped across the room, grabbed the chair from in front of the door and, as Hughie recovered himself and lunged forward, hurled it at him with all his might. There was a *thunk* as it caught him on the side of the head and the shoulder. The big man went down on his knees.

Bill Davidson waited to see no more. He wrenched open the door, leapt out of the Portakabin, sprinted over the track and down the far bank, then fled as fast his legs would carry him across the darkening moorland.

A minute later Hughie stumbled out, rubbing his head. He leant against the side of the Portakabin, took several deep breaths and raised the rifle to his shoulder, squinting through the telescopic sight as he swept it back and forth across the open ground in front of the quarry. After a while he nodded to himself in satisfaction, steadied the weapon and fired.

It was a long shot and it went wide, but not that wide. Snow plumed off a clump of heather a few feet to Bill Davidson's right. He glanced over his shoulder and increased his speed. Within a few seconds he was out of range.

Hughie lowered the rifle. Unhurriedly, he bent down to check his bootlaces. Then, with a loping, confident stride, he set off in pursuit.

Christie listened to the engine ticking over and stared dully at the snowflakes floating through the gloom outside. What was going on up there, she wondered. Warm and relatively safe as she was here in the car, she was conscious nonetheless of a growing restlessness which was telling her that it wasn't enough just to have sent someone else to try and intervene: she needed to be there herself. In fact she badly wanted to be there herself.

She glanced across at her grandmother who had sunk down in the driver's seat. Although her hands still rested on the wheel, her eyelids fluttered and it was clear that she was struggling to stay awake. But she sensed Christie's attention and looked up with an exhausted smile.

'Are you all right, dear?'

'Yes, Nan, I'm fine. Are you OK?' Christie returned the smile.

'Yes . . . but I seem to be nodding off. Maybe we should turn the heater down a bit.'

'No, we'll freeze. But don't worry. I'm not going to sleep. I'll let you know as soon as anything happens.'

'All right, dear.' A moment later her eyes closed.

Christie waited a couple of minutes, then felt for the door handle and pressed gently down. Janet's car was new and the door opened soundlessly but a freezing draught slid in and her grandmother shivered and opened one eye.

'Just going to the loo!' said Christie, surprised and a little guilty at how easily the lie came.

Her grandmother nodded drowsily.

Christie slipped out and closed the door quickly. She went round to the back of the car, checked that her grandmother wasn't watching, then ducked down and crossed the road. Once in the wood she began to climb as fast as she could, dodging between the trees and ignoring the brambles that scraped at her legs. Eventually the dim shapes of Neil and Tom became visible against their trees, the open ground beyond.

As she drew closer, Neil scrambled to his feet and levelled the gun.

'It's all right,' she panted in a half-whisper. 'It's me, Christie.'

'God you gave me a fright, lassie,' said Neil, lowering the gun again. 'But look, you shouldn't be . . .'

A distant rifle-shot echoed across the hillside. Before the sound had died away Tom flung out his arm in the direction of the quarry-hill.

'Look! Over there!'

Visibility was now minimal and for some moments Christie strained her eyes through the snow-streaked gloom. Then, with a sudden tightening in her chest, she caught sight of a small, lonely figure weaving its way through the desolate landscape.

As if connected by some invisible umbilicus, Christie could almost feel the fear, the exhaustion, as she watched it lurch across the heather, tripping and stumbling.

For several seconds it disappeared behind a hummock and as it re-appeared, Tom called out again:

'Behind him! Do you see?'

She glanced back towards the hill, her eyes acclimatising now to the dusk, and shortly caught sight of a larger figure covering the ground with the lolloping gait of a long-distance runner. A rifle hung loosely from one hand.

Bill Davidson was now halfway between the quarry and the stone and his pace was slowing. Little by little his pursuer was gaining on him.

Christie heard Neil getting to his feet and slipping the safety catch on the shotgun but she did not, could not, take her eyes off the chase.

'Not yet, Neil!' she called across to him. 'I'll say when.' Something was telling her to leave it till the last possible moment.

Once again Bill Davidson disappeared into a stretch of dead ground. His pursuer at the same time went behind the hummock. Christie's heart pounded as she waited for the fugitive to re-appear.

Seconds passed and his pursuer emerged from behind the

hummock but still there was no sign of Bill Davidson. Then, to her horror, she saw his pursuer drop to one knee in the snow and raise the rifle to his shoulder. A moment later Bill Davidson came into view at the foot of the escarpment, beneath the big stone.

He was struggling now to keep his pace and Christie found her own breath coming short and shallow as she watched him labouring up the slope. She could stand it no longer.

'Now!' she shouted to Neil.

There was a dull *click, click* as the firing pins struck the percussion caps. The gun had failed to go off.

For a moment Christie's head swam with panic. Then, as Neil fumbled to reload the gun, she broke from the cover of the trees and ran blindly out onto the heather, waving her arms and yelling at the top of her voice.

She saw the gunman lift his head and glance briefly in her direction, then return his cheek to the stock of his rifle. But her cries had their effect on Bill Davidson who had now reached the top of the escarpment. He stopped for a moment by the stone and turned towards her. At that moment there was the sharp crack of the rifle. He lurched backwards, flinging out his arms and toppled from view.

It seemed to Christie as if time were suspended. There was nothing but the soughing of the snow-laden wind as she stared, horror-stricken, at the empty space through which Bill Davidson's limp body had briefly tumbled.

Then several things happened at once.

With an agonised cry of 'Dad!', Tom raced out from the trees, heading for the unseen foot of the escarpment. At the same time Neil yelled 'Get down!' and an instant later there was a second shot. Something zinged over Christie's head as she turned dreamily to look at the gunman who had swivelled to the right and now had his weapon trained directly on her. Then a heavy body crashed on top of her, flinging her down into the heather where she struggled briefly to clear the snow from her mouth and nostrils and lay still, the image of Bill Davidson's falling figure still burning in her mind's eye.

There was a third shot and an almost simultaneous yell of pain from the body on top of her. Then a new sound intruded: a regular mechanical thud-thud, thud-thud, growing louder and faster until it was the clearly identifiable roar of helicopter rotors. A hugely amplified voice rang across the moorland:

'This is the police! Drop your weapon. I repeat, police! Drop your weapon!'

The smothering weight slowly removed itself from her back and she climbed unsteadily to her feet to see the helicopter hovering above the gunman who was standing motionless with his hands raised in the centre of a wide circle of flattened heather from whose edges the snow whipped away as if in a blizzard. Twin spotlights stabbed the gloom to illuminate him like an immense bearded dummy in some deserted corner of a waxworks.

The helicopter crabbed to the right and landed. Its doors flew open and two plain-clothes policemen dashed forward, heads bent, to pinion the gunman. He offered no resistance as they marched him towards the helicopter and handcuffed him to one of the skids. Then they made their way over to Christie and Neil who was standing beside her with one hand to his left shoulder, his face creased with pain. Sirens and blue flashing lights, away to their left, announced the arrival of more police at the quarry.

'Damp cartridges!' Neil muttered to himself, shaking his head as the plain-clothesmen approached. They were only a few yards off when there came a cry from the rising ground which concealed the foot of the escarpment. The two policemen spun round as Tom appeared, waving and shouting: 'Over here! Quick!'

'It's OK, he's with us,' Neil called to the policemen as they turned and began to sprint in Tom's direction. He and Christie followed.

As they reached the top of the rise the ground fell away to

reveal the cliff edge of the escarptment, dropping thirty feet sheer from beneath *Morag Dubh*, who now sat with her back turned to them. Stretching away from the foot of the cliff towards a little loch was a region of flat ground hatched with peat-hags. Up to his shoulders in one of these hags, close in under the cliff, stood Tom, beckoning urgently.

By the time Neil and Christie arrived the two plain-clothesmen were already down in the hag beside Tom. Bill Davidson lay sprawled across its black, silty floor. One of the men was on his knees examining him. Tom's face was white and pinched with anxiety.

At length the man stood up.

'He's taken a shot in the shoulder and he has a broken leg and some broken ribs, probably from the fall. He's alive but we'll need to get him straight to hospital.' He looked up at Neil and caught sight of his clasped arm and pained expression: 'Are you OK?'

Neil nodded. 'Just grazed, I think,' he replied through clenched teeth.

'Then if you wouldn't mind waiting here, we'll fetch a stretcher.'

A couple of minutes later they returned and rolled the still-unconscious form onto the stretcher. Christie, Tom and Neil accompanied them back to the helicopter and watched as they loaded it in, then unshackled Wee Hughie from the skid and prodded him inside also.

'Sergeant Drummond will be over from the quarry in a minute. You can start making your way back there if you want,' said one of the policemen, leaning from the cockpit. He made to close the door, then thought of something and added: 'Your friend was helluva lucky you were there, you know. We might very easily not have found him down in that hag and he certainly wouldn't have lasted the night in his condition.'

He closed the door and Christie, Tom and Neil backed away as the engine started up again and the rotors began to swing. When the noise reached a deafening roar and the down-draught buffeted their heads, the helicopter lifted off and thudded away into the now almost total darkness.

The three of them turned round and set off back towards the quarry, from which torchlights were beginning to wink across the moorland.

Christie felt shocked and quite disconnected with her surroundings. She was scarcely even aware of her feet making contact with the ground as she plodded across the heather with only one set of thoughts swirling round and round like dragonsmoke in her brain:

The voice she had heard in the vision in the cave, the voice that had caused Bill Davidson to stop at the critical moment, the voice that had given the gunman a stationary target — that voice had been her own!

Chapter 13

By the time the CID inspector arrived from Inverness it was ten o'clock.

They had been in the sitting room at the cottage for an hour and a half — Christie, her grandmother, Tom and PC McDonald from Aultbea. Neil was over at the doctor's house having his arm attended to.

The fire was blazing and the little room had become so warm that it was all Christie could do to keep her eyes open. She was grateful for the exhaustion that had finally overwhelmed her as they had been driven back from the quarry in a police car. It seemed to have deadened the shock and slowed down her mind, blurring the awful discovery she had made: she could hardly even remember what it had been, now.

When it came to her turn to tell the inspector what had happened she repeated the story mechanically, incapable any longer of reliving its emotion in the telling. It was just a hunch, she explained, that had taken them to *Morag Dubh*. She noticed the inspector raise an eyebrow and she also noticed her grandmother catch his eye. Something unspoken passed between them, but she was too tired to care what.

As she finished, Neil returned and began to give his version of events. Her grandmother excused them both and led her upstairs, helped her to undress and tucked her up in bed. She was asleep before the door closed.

Sometime after eleven the next morning she awoke to hear her grandmother enter the bedroom and draw the curtains. A shaft of brilliant sunlight flooded in as Christie lifted her head from the pillow and looked across at four square panes of clear blue sky.

Her grandmother sat down on the edge of the bed and held out the *Ullapool Courier* for her inspection. Beside a two-column photograph of Bill Davidson was the headline: *Alba Nova boss foils PAA terror attempt.*

'It would seem he's had his cake and eaten it!' said her grandmother with a wry smile. 'I can't say he deserved it.'

'How is he?' asked Christie.

'Neil was going to ring the hospital this morning — once they've got the wires back up. We'll go over later and find out.'

'So they got the others?' asked Christie, too sleepy yet to read the article.

'Yes. They got them last night. Don't you remember the inspector telling us?'

Christie shook her head. She seemed to have little recollection of anything at the moment.

'The police had a nice wee reception committee waiting for them at the fuel depot.'

Christie fell back on the pillow and closed her eyes. 'So that's it, then.'

'Yes, dear. That's it, thank goodness. Now we can all get back to normal.' She sat in silence for a while, eyeing her granddaughter affectionately. Christie stared at the window as the memories slowly returned.

'You're . . . you're not cross with me . . . for running off?' she asked at length.

Her grandmother shook her head. 'I was at the time . . . but not now.'

'You see I had to be there . . .' Christie began, then stopped, feeling suddenly shaky, close to tears.

Her grandmother waited patiently for her to continue.

'. . . because . . . well . . . I saw everything exactly as I'd seen it in the cave, but there was one thing I hadn't realised. It was *my* voice that made him stop. You see, Nan, I'd gone there to try and change what was going to happen but in fact I *had* to be there *for* it to happen. I was part of it all along!'

Her grandmother did not answer immediately. She reached out and clasped her granddaughter's hand on the counterpane, then said slowly:

'That's called destiny, Christie. There is a belief that we all have a destiny. It's not such a terrible thing.'

'But it means it was my fault he was shot,' said Christie miserably. 'Why would my destiny plan something like that for me?'

Her grandmother smiled. 'Because if you hadn't been there he might have been killed. As it was he was only wounded. Or he might have been wounded and left to die on the hillside. Either way, dear, it was your being there that *saved* him, do you see? And that was why it was your destiny not only to see it but to be part of it!'

'Oh,' said Christie, feeling the stirring of a great wave of relief. 'I hadn't thought of that.' Gradually she broke into a smile. She leant forward and hugged her grandmother.

'There's something else, too,' said her grandmother after a while.

'What's that, Nan?'

'Mr Davidson wasn't actually murdered, was he?'

'No.'

'So you're going to have to learn not to jump to conclusions about what you see.'

'Especially when I can't change anything.'

'Especially when you can't change anything.'

*

After Christie had breakfasted they went next-door. Neil was at the stove and Tom, who had slept in Neil's spare bedroom, was busying himself with an enormous plate of sausages and baked beans.

'The laddie's got a worm, I'm sure of it,' said Neil, looking up and grinning as they entered. Apart from a bulge under his sweater where his arm was bandaged, he appeared none the worse for his experience.

Tom still looked a little paler than usual but his appetite suggested that he was well on the way to recovery.

Christie sat down beside him and showed him the *Ullapool Courier*.

'Jammy so-and-so!' he commented, looking at the photo of his father. There was a hint of something, almost pride, in his voice, thought Christie.

'Well,' he continued, still chewing, 'I'm not going to tell them anything different!'

'Nor I,' she agreed thankfully. The idea of having to explain what had actually happened to anyone, let alone a reporter, made her feel sick with embarrassment. 'Anyway, how is he?'

'He's fine,' Neil replied. 'He's going to have to stay in hospital a while. But there's nothing they can't put right.'

'Tough as old boots!' mumbled Tom through a mouthful of toast.

A little later the four of them went across to the cabin to pack up Tom's and his father's belongings. As Christie scooped up the papers in the sitting room she found her mind returning to the first evening she had come to the cabin and seen Bill Davidson, Dougal Mackay and Bertie Ross sitting around the table. Two-and-half days ago. It seemed like a year.

And what would become of Alba Nova, she wondered, pausing with the glossy green and gold brochure in one hand. Probably continue as if nothing had ever happened, judging from what she had come to learn of Bill Davidson.

Still, as Tom had said, he did seem to believe in some important things . . .

When they were through they stacked Bill Davidson's possessions by the door, ready to be loaded into the Range Rover once it had been released by the police forensic team. Tom's belongings they placed in Janet's car and after Tom had said goodbye to Neil, he, Christie and her grandmother set off for Inverness.

As they turned left at Laide and onto the main road, swinging along the curve of Gruinard Bay, Christie glanced out across the gently ruffled blue water. In the far distance the high hills glistened under their new coating of snow, but the lower ground showed not a trace of the cold weather of the past few days. The grass seemed brilliantly green, the heather was beginning to come alive like the spring coat of a young stag and even Gruinard Island seemed to have been warmed in some indefinable way by the sunlight.

Christie fished in her pocket and pulled out a tape.

'Do you mind, Nan?' she asked.

'Of course not!' said her grandmother.

She slipped it into the tape deck and turned round to catch Tom's look of pleasure as The Bothy Boys' rich harmonies and foot-tapping fiddles and guitars swept them into the Lewis Bridal song:

> Step we gaily, on we go
> Heel for heel and toe for toe
> Arm in arm and row on row
> All for Mairi's wedding . . .

In Bill Davidson's hospital room a woman reporter was sitting at his bedside, scribbling in a notebook. He was smiling at her, almost flirtatiously, as he answered her questions; she was nodding respectfully and attentively at the end of the each sentence. It was obvious that he needed little encouragement to repeat his story.

As Tom, Christie and her grandmother entered he looked

up and an awkward frown crossed his face, but it escaped the notice of the reporter who was already on her feet, thrusting out her hand to all three of them at once.

'Aha!' she said with the air of a bloodhound catching scent. 'The rest of the terrorist-trappers! Maureen MacIver of the *Press and Journal*! Can I ask you a few questions?'

Christie's heart sank but her grandmother stepped in immediately: 'I'm sure Mr Davidson has told you all you need to know.'

The swiftness of her reply and her tone of voice made it quite clear that members of the press could expect not an ounce of co-operation from her.

The reporter blinked and fumbled with her notebook. Then she recovered herself and turned to Bill Davidson.

'Well Mr Davidson, you've given me plenty to go on. Thank you *very* much!' Her voice was oily with admiration. 'I hope you have a speedy recovery and please keep me in touch with all your Alba Nova developments. You can count on my support.' She left the room.

'Bloody press!' said Bill Davidson with feigned distaste. 'They've been in and out all morning.' He paused for a moment, glancing at his visitors, then continued, somewhat gruffly: 'Well, come in, come in!'

He was dressed in a pair of striped hospital pyjamas. One leg was encased in plaster and raised up on a frame at the end of the bed. His torso was swathed with bandages as was his right shoulder. A drip was taped to his left wrist.

'Are you all right, Dad?' asked Tom anxiously.

'I'll live, son.' His reply was terse and he appeared almost embarrassed, thought Christie. She noticed that he was studiously avoiding direct eye contact with any of them.

There was another moment's uncomfortable silence before he waved at a couple of armchairs and said: 'Have a seat, then.'

Christie and her grandmother took the armchairs and Tom made for the reporter's place at his father's bedside.

'So, then,' said Christie's grandmother with a pleasant

smile. 'All's well that ends well, it seems.'

Bill Davidson looked at her with the same awkward frown.

'Yes, Mrs McKenzie. But we know that all is not quite as it seems. I'll admit I've been lucky that the press have decided to go for . . . a certain version of events. That still leaves me with the tricky question of where I stand in relation to you three.' His voice was quite unemotional, as if he was dealing with a business problem rather than a question of personal honour.

'Tut tut, Mr Davidson,' said Christie's grandmother, still smiling. 'It's over. We're best to forget the whole thing.'

'That's very generous,' he replied without returning her smile. 'But it's easier for you than for me. I'm the one that made a fool of myself.'

'Come on, Dad, we all make mis . . .' Tom began, but his father interjected curtly: 'No need to soft soap me, son! I know damn well how badly I got it wrong . . .' He stared at the bedspread, unsure of what to say next.

Christie's grandmother broke the silence. 'Well, I suppose,' she suggested mildly, 'you might feel a little better if you apologised.'

Christie held her breath, waiting for the outburst as Bill Davidson's jaw dropped in amazement. But to her great surprise it did not come.

He looked down and for a long time studied the backs of his hands. Then slowly, as if in the grip of a revelation, he said: 'Yes . . . I suppose I could.' There was a hint of warmth creeping into his voice. He nodded to himself and continued: 'OK, I do . . . I apologise . . . to all of you.' He looked at each of them in turn and when his gaze fell on Christie she saw, for the first time, a corresponding glimmer of warmth in the normally cold blue eyes. It was as if she were looking at a completely different man — a man who could very easily have once looked a lot like Tom.

'And . . .' he hesitated, still holding her gaze, 'I'm told that you somehow managed to be on hand when that thug started taking potshots at me, and that if you hadn't been there I would more than likely have been killed, or left on the hillside to die. I don't know how you managed it, Christie, but I'd like you to know that I'm very grateful to you. In fact,' he turned to the others, 'I'm grateful to all of you.'

He fell silent for a moment, then cleared his throat sharply, as if to bring his emotions under control. 'If there's ever anything I can do for you, Christie . . . Mrs McKenzie, you're to let me know.' His voice was brisk again.

'That's most kind of you,' said Christie's grandmother, 'but quite unnecessary. We're all just glad it's over. Now, I think we should leave you. You've had quite a time of it and I expect you need some rest.' She rose from her chair.

Christie followed suit and Tom began to get to his feet but his father motioned him down again.

'I'd like a few words with you, Tom,' he said.

Christie noticed Tom's worried look. She caught his eye and gave him an encouraging wink as she followed her grandmother to the door.

Her grandmother paused with her hand on the handle and turned round with a final smile. 'Goodbye, Mr Davidson.'

'Goodbye, Mrs McKenzie . . . and Christie . . . will we be seeing you again?'

'I don't know,' said Christie, following her grandmother out of the room.

As the door closed behind them, Christie and her grandmother exchanged glances.

'He wasn't just putting it on, was he?' said Christie.

Her grandmother shook her head.

'But do you think he'll go on being . . . well . . . different, from now on?'

Her grandmother studied the floor for a moment before looking up at Christie and replying:

'That I couldn't say, dear. I really couldn't say.'

*

A few minutes later Tom emerged into the corridor. He looked a little dazed as he sat down on the bench beside them.

'Well?' asked Christie, dying to know what had taken place.

'Well,' said Tom at length, 'it looks as if I've got myself a band.'

'What do you mean . . . a band?'

'A band. Music. He's offered to buy all the equipment if I can get the right people together . . . mikes . . . amps . . . a PA system . . .'

'Wow, that's amazing!' said Christie.

'And . . . you'll never believe this . . .' his dazed look was rapidly changing to one of delight, 'he's said when we're up to scratch he'll manage us . . . get us bookings for gigs . . . you see, Davidson Holdings isn't just farming, it owns clubs, camping sites, hotels . . . he can get us in all over the place!'

'That's wonderful. Tom! You deserve it!' said Christie's grandmother getting to her feet. 'Now, we'd better get a move on or we'll miss your train.'

'But why?' asked Christie as they made their way to the lift. 'I mean . . . why the sudden generosity?'

'He didn't really say,' Tom replied, 'but I guess it's to . . . kind of . . . make up for everything that's happened.'

A sudden sour thought intruded and before she could check herself, Christie had given voice to it: 'You don't think he's just making sure that you never let on what really happened.'

'I can't be certain,' he replied thoughtfully, 'but I don't think so. There was something different about him in there.'

Christie nodded, 'I noticed it too.'

The lift arrived and they pressed the button for the car park.

'So he's decided to take your music seriously?' Christie asked as the doors closed.

'It seems so,' Tom replied.

'Things are changing, then.'

'Maybe.'

'Do you know what I say, Tom Davidson?'

'What's that?'

'I say three cheers for the People's Army of Albatross!'

'Hip, hip, hooray!' said Tom, striding from the lift. He began to whistle as they crossed the car park.

At the station, Tom went off to buy his ticket while Christie and her grandmother found a trolley and wheeled his luggage along to the platform where the Perth train was waiting.

He was gone for some while and when he returned he was clutching a bunch of daffodils which he thrust awkwardly at Christie's grandmother with a muttered 'Thanks for everything'. His confusion was increased when she leant forward and kissed him lightly on the cheek.

'You're a dear lad, Tom,' she said.

He climbed into the train and they handed him up his bags. Finally Christie passed him the guitar case.

'We didn't get much singing done, did we,' she said sadly.

'No,' he replied with a broad grin. 'But we will.'

Christie gave him quizzical look.

'I don't think Dad'll expect me to go fishing with him again . . .' he said obliquely. There was a wicked glint in his eyes, as if he was willing Christie to guess what he was leading up to.

'So?' said Christie, hardly able to bear the suspense.

'So, I'll be making my own plans for next holidays . . .'

'And . . . ?'

'And . . . I thought . . . maybe . . . you'd like come and stay for bit?'

For a moment Christie was unable to find her words, but at last, sounding a little strangled, she said:

'Oh yes, Tom! That would be brilliant!' She glanced anxiously at her grandmother and added: 'I'll have to ask Mum and Dad, of course.'

'I'm sure that won't be a problem, dear,' said her

grandmother, smiling quietly. 'I'll see to it.'

'We'll write a . . . whaddo-they-call-it . . . theme song for Alba Nova,' said Tom.

'OK,' said Christie, feeling suddenly weak with excitement. She lowered her eyes as the colour raced to her cheeks, and at that moment there was a hiss of releasing brakes. The train began to pull away.

'Till the summer, then!' called Tom, leaning out of the window and waving until a bend in the track took him from view.

Christie and her grandmother walked back to the car in silence.

'You'll be ready for the quiet life in Mallaig after all this!' said her grandmother as they left Inverness and passed beneath the southern tower of the Kessock Bridge. The waters of the Beauly Firth glinted in the sunlight beneath them.

'Mmmm,' said Christie, 'I suppose I will. But it's been a great holiday, Nan. I wouldn't have missed it for anything.'

She settled back in her seat and gazed ahead at the distant westerly hills, rising like slumbering giants beyond the flat lands of the Black Isle and Dingwall. There was one more thing she had to do still . . .

She closed her eyes and allowed her mind to travel down through the labyrinth of passages to the dark lair in her deepest, innermost place. The dragon was there, snorting gently. She went towards him and he did not move until she was right in front of him. Then, slowly, ponderously, he lifted his head so that she could look straight up his long scaly snout and into his eyes.

They were green, like the rest of him, but there the similarity ceased. For his eyes had the liquescence of deep, dimly-lit subterranean pools in which glimmered together an immeasurable wisdom, an unquenchable rage, an infinite compassion and a perpetual wry amusement.

For some time Christie allowed herself to swim in their depths. Then she stepped back, drew herself up and said to him: 'If you're going to let me get at that treasure, we're going to have to learn to be friends, aren't we?'

The dragon did not reply.

He did not even move his head.

There was just the flicker of one horny green eyelid in a barely perceptible wink.